The Fisherman's Daughter

Sydell Lowell Voeller

Published by Sydell Voeller, 2023.

This is a work of fiction. Similarities to real people, places, or events are entirely coincidental.

THE FISHERMAN'S DAUGHTER

First edition. September 15, 2023.

Copyright © 2023 Sydell Lowell Voeller.

ISBN: 979-8223872474

Written by Sydell Lowell Voeller.

Also by Sydell Lowell Voeller

Her Sister's Keeper
The Heart Leads Home
The Fisherman's Daughter

Watch for more at sydellvoeller.com.

Chapter One

Sea spray cooled Vanessa Paris's cheeks as she gazed from the ferry across the froth-tipped waves of Puget Sound. *Missing.* The words gouged deep into her mind. How could Dad have disappeared from his small fishing boat without leaving a clue? The desperate call from Clinton Paris, her father's brother, had come only last night.

That morning she'd hastily arranged for a leave-of-absence at the university in Seattle where she taught as an assistant professor in the psychology department. The afternoon drive up the Interstate to the ferry terminal had seemed to take forever. At last she was almost home.

Raising a hand to shield her eyes from the sun, she watched the approaching craggy shore, edged with a saw tooth line of dark evergreens. Tawanya Island. The northern-most of the San Juan Islands. Her childhood home.

Thoughts of her father resurfaced and a pang shot through her. What if he was never found? What if he'd fallen overboard, was knocked unconscious, and sank beneath the frigid waters?

Vanessa gave a quick shake of her head. No, that just couldn't happen. Dad was an expert fisherman. He'd always believed in his abilities, just as he'd taught her to believe in hers. Everyone on the entire island agreed that Eldon Paris was a master of the sea. Nearly every day at the Kaloch Bay Lodge, owned and operated by her father and uncle, Dad would fire up the engine of the "Lady Luck" and welcome the hopeful tourists who'd signed on for his guided fishing expeditions.

Overhead, a seagull screeched, momentarily breaking into her anxious thoughts. The last rays of an early summer sun were quickly fading beyond the horizon. In the distance, white sails billowed against the sky.

Vanessa lifted her chin. Yes, Dad would want her to be brave. She was not only homeward bound, but bound in her love for him. She had no choice but to unravel the mystery of his disappearance.

*****

"Are you sure Dad left alone?" Vanessa questioned her uncle after exchanging quick hugs. She followed Clinton through the hall foyer and into the rustic lobby of Kaloch Bay Lodge. "Why didn't he go with Matt Redding? They've fished together for at least fifteen years now."

"Matt couldn't go with him. Your pop left two days ago at the crack of dawn, and I'm sure he was alone. Said he wanted some time for a day of trawling and he'd be back no later than seven."

She ran a trembling hand through her long, dark brown hair and shook her head. "Dad should've never done it. He's got a heart condition."

"That's not the way Eldon sees it," he replied. "As long as his old ticker keeps on a tickin', your pop's gonna do exactly as he pleases. And you, my dear niece, in all your twenty-five years of livin', you should know him as well as I do." Clinton stooped to stoke up the embers in the huge stone fireplace, then tossed on another log.

"I'm afraid you're right." As the flames sputtered and crackled, warmth wrapped around her, yet it failed to thaw the icy cold fear deep inside of her. She sank into her favorite leather armchair as her uncle seated himself across from her.

"It's not that he wouldn't have welcomed Matt's company," Clinton went on. "Lately Eldon's been complainin' that Matt's been too damned busy for his own good."

A commotion in the foyer interrupted him and he rose wearily. "Probably another one of those Coast Guard investigators or maybe someone from the sheriff's department. They've been dropping in all day. Oh, it's not that I don't appreciate what they're trying to do, mind you. It's just that they keep asking the same questions over and over." He patted her shoulder. "Hold on, kiddo. I'll be back as soon as I can."

She sprang up "Wait up! I'm coming too!

When she arrived in the foyer, her uncle and two blue uniformed Coast Guard officers were engaged in intense conversation. The taller man appeared to be in his early twenties, the other closer to middle-age.

"We've found Mr. Paris's boat up near the North Spit and immediately mounted a search," the older officer was saying. "The engine was still idling, the autopilot switched on and the refrigerator fully stocked." He slanted a glance at Clinton. "Can you tell me about your brother's emotional state? Was he depressed? Acting strange?"

"Dad's no different than anyone else," Vanessa broke in. "Oh, by the way, I'm Vanessa Paris, his only daughter. What I'm trying to say is, he may have his ups and downs sometimes, but who doesn't?" If they were considering that Dad had purposefully drowned himself, they were wrong. Dad's robust love of life would never give way to suicide.

"What about his heart medication?" she continued. "Did you find it on board?"

"Yes," he answered. "The two half-empty bottles were uncapped, sitting on the galley table."

Vanessa brushed back a tear. The picture of her father's deserted boat was too much to bear. If he had left it, knowing he'd be gone for more than a day, why didn't he take his pills with him?

"Did my brother radio in a Mayday?" Clinton asked.

"No sir. None at all."

Several lodge guests gathered around, yet as Vanessa's attention narrowed on the younger officer's next words, the guests' faces blurred into obscurity. "We've suspended the search for the night, but will continue sending out more helicopters and cutters tomorrow. In the meantime, we're holding Mr. Paris's boat at our operations center on Bradshaw Island. We'll let you know as soon as anything turns up."

"Is there anything we can do?" Vanessa pleaded. Though just being back on the island made her feel closer to her father, she knew that wasn't enough. She must get involved with the search. And if the authorities weren't about to suggest a way, she'd find her own.

The best thing you can do is stand by for further questioning," the other officer answered. "We have a very competent search and rescue team. Rest assured we're doing everything possible." With that, the two men made a hasty exit out the door.

The landline telephone in the office jangled, and Clinton dashed to answer it as Vanessa wandered back into the lobby to escape the curious stares of the guests. Maybe tomorrow she could face them, but not yet. Fatigue weighted her feet.

A blast of cool air gusted from the back of the room. Turning on her heel, Vanessa stared at the tall, well-built masculine figure that filled the doorway leading onto the deck.

"Lowell Maxwell!" she exclaimed. Recognition rocked her. She reached quickly to clasp the back of a chair in an effort to steady herself. Eleven years ago, he and her older brother, Andrew, had been the best of friends. Lowell had spent many a weekend hanging out with Andy here at the lodge. Vanessa, completely smitten by Lowell's blond good looks, had invented every excuse imaginable to try to get his attention.

"Yep, it's been a long time, hasn't it? I was standing outside," he said huskily. His gaze locked with hers. "I couldn't help overhearing your conversation. How're you doing, Vanessa? Are you holding up okay?"

"Yes, no." Her heart raced as she groped for a sane reply. Lowell had grown more handsome than she'd ever dreamed possible. He stood tall, broad-shouldered and powerfully masculine. But she mustn't let him get to her, she quickly cautioned herself.

No, she simply must not.

People you loved, people you trusted, only ended up dying.

"The news about Dad came as quite a shock, of course," she finally continued, taking a cautious step backward. "Somehow I keep telling myself there must be a mistake. That they mistook Dad's boat for someone else's. That any moment now he'll appear out of nowhere." She sighed, blinking rapidly to keep from crying. "And what about you, Lowell? Are you here on vacation?"

"I'm not a guest, Vanessa. I work here."

"I don't understand. Clinton never mentioned—"

"I suppose not," he interrupted, raking his hand through sandy-blond hair. "He's quite shaken now about your father too. So am I." He paused, then jerked his head towards the deck. "Let's go outside where we can talk more privately."

She hesitated. "All right." She wasn't sure why, but Lowell seemed steeled by his own brand of caution. The tension stretching between them was so palpable she could almost reach out and touch it.

They sat, she sinking into a webbed lawn chair, he hitching himself onto a stool alongside of her. For a long while, they stared out at the bay, neither speaking, neither daring to look at each other.

"When I first came back to the islands, I felt as if I'd been away forever," Lowell said, finally breaking the silence. He leaned forward, studying the back of his hand.

"Eleven years *is* a long time," she agreed softly.

"Yep. Eleven years and three months since I left for Oregon State and Andy enlisted with the Navy."

"And so much has happened." Her voice trailed. Unbidden, the memories washed over her.

Lowell. The rebel of Tawanya High with his devil-may-care grin and his tough kid airs. Lowell had been the only boy who'd managed to steal her heart, though they'd never even once gone out on a date. Much to her bitter disappointment, her crush on him had remained totally one-sided.

Just as well, her mother had often said. Lowell was four years older, a senior, and far too worldly for Vanessa. What's more, he drove his car much too fast. Wore his jeans much too tight. It didn't matter that Andy did too, Mama had replied each time Vanessa pointed out the obvious. Vanessa needed to stick with boys closer to her own age.

Vanessa forced her attention back to the present. "So exactly when *did* you arrive?" she asked. What kind of work are you doing here?"

"I came back a month ago. My brother Sam—the only brother who still lives here on the island—is letting me stay on his sailboat, which I'm keeping docked in your harbor. He and Miranda, his new wife, invited me to move in with them." He turned to look at her. His face remained closed and tight. "But I turned them down. I needed my own space. Time alone. Time to sort things out."

"I see," she said. *My own space. Time alone.* No, she didn't see at all. Lowell had always run with the coolest crowd at school. He'd never been a loner. Questions tumbled inside her mind. Was he running away from something? A broken relationship perhaps?

"So what has Clinton has hired you to do?" she asked, struggling to sound nonchalant. His physical nearness was threatening to rip her resolve into a thousand shreds.

"Your *father* and Clinton," he corrected her. "I'm freelancing as a handyman. I plan to take on as much work as I have time for, not only here, but for some of the other lodge owners in the islands too."

"So you're a teacher then?" she asked. Who else had summers free other than teachers and ski lift operators?

"No. I'm a cop." His gaze moved fleetingly over her, then came to rest again on her face. "I'm here on a temporary leave from my job in L.A. Four more weeks."

"A cop," she repeated, meeting his stunningly blue eyes, noting the breeze rippling through his hair. He certainly fit the stereotype. Broad shouldered and strong. Opened black leather jacket with the collar turned up. An incredible heart-stopper with his sophisticated good looks. But cops were the worst choice for a husband—if she were looking for one, which she definitely was not. Cops lived in the fast track. With violence. And danger. Cops were gunned down every day.

"What happened?" she asked him. "What happened in L.A. to make you need to get away?"

He averted his gaze. "It's too personal to talk about. Let's talk about you."

She felt her hands trembling, but couldn't seem to will them to stop. So far neither of them had mentioned Andy, though she sensed he wanted to.

"Tell me more about your work," he urged quickly. "Eldon said you're a shrink."

She chuckled in spite of herself. "Leave it to Dad to get things a little mixed up. Though that's my goal, right now I'm an assistant professor at the University of Washington. I teach psychology and head up a support group for troubled teens."

He quirked an eyebrow, the hint of a smile playing on his face. "I guess it fits."

"Meaning?"

"Meaning you're apparently still the crusader you were back during high school. Clean-up the beaches. Save the whales. Only now you're rescuing people instead."

"And as *I* remember, you used to say you never had time for causes."

"I still don't. Some things never change." He shifted his weight. "Hard work. Sweat and tears. That's the bottom line. Right, Vanessa?"

"Uh . . . of course." My, he certainly had a grim way of looking at things, she thought. And what about his evasiveness when he'd talked about his leave from his job? Was it too soon to expect him to confide in her? *Would he ever?*

As if reading her thoughts, he got to his feet. "It's been a long day for both of us. Too long. Time to go."

"Yes." She rose also, though something deep inside of her yearned to prolong their conversation. For an immeasurable moment, they simply stood there, assessing each other, their gazes locked.

"It's great seeing you again," Lowell said at last, his voice gruff with emotion.

"Good seeing you too."

Smiling, he reached out and touched her shoulder, allowing his hand to linger just a little too long.

Her pulse raced. She felt breathless and light headed.

"'Night, Vanessa."

"Good night, Lowell."

He turned to leave, then paused for a second, tossing a look over his shoulder.

"Sleep well," she called after him.

"I'll try to. You too."

As she watched him disappear down the flight of stairs leading down from the deck to the lower yard, she exhaled slowly. At last. Now that he was safely out of sight, she could let her guard down. Her nerves were stretched as tight as a guitar string.

She couldn't help wondering whether Andrew had ever told Lowell about her crush on him. Hopefully he had not, because she certainly wasn't going to give him any encouragement now. Moreover, as far as her brother was concerned, she would never know the answer to that question. Andy, who'd later decided to make the Navy his career, had been killed in a car accident three years ago. Hugging her arms to her chest, she wandered back inside. She could still almost feel where Lowell had touched her shoulder, and for a foolish moment, wondered whether his lips against hers would feel every bit as exquisite.

"Yes, Ruby, Vanessa arrived safely." The sound of Clinton still talking on the phone sliced through her thoughts.

Vanessa smiled, knowing the elderly lady would probably keep her uncle on the line as long as possible. Ruby had not only been a close family friend for a long time, but also Vanessa's piano teacher. A widow for ten years now, she'd taken a special interest in Clinton, who'd claimed to be a confirmed bachelor.

As Vanessa waited for her uncle to hang up the phone, her gaze swept the lobby. The large room had always been the heart of the lodge where guests had gathered in the evening to read and visit, or in the early gray dawn, preparing to leave on a guided fishing trip.

Before Vanessa was old enough to attend the island grade school, her mother had sometimes allowed her to play in the lobby while she managed the front office. Ragtime, the pet calico cat, usually purred loudly from her favorite spot on the Navajo throw rug by the fireplace. The guests seemed to appreciate these homey touches, and her mother had said that Vanessa's constant exposure to a variety of people helped mold her into the loving, generous young lady she was quickly becoming.

Mama, Vanessa thought with bittersweet pain. Everywhere she looked reminders of her mother seeped through. She wandered over to the pine-drop table, touching it reverently. Mama had refinished it with loving patience. On the far wall shelf stood her hand-woven baskets, her collection of Indian artifacts. Mama had preceded Andrew in death by only one year, a victim of cancer.

Stifling a yawn, she heard Clinton's footsteps growing louder as he crossed the hall to the lobby.

"Ruby sends her regards," he said, taking a long slow draw on his pipe. The sweet aroma of cherry tobacco wafted about them, mixing with the mouth-watering smells that drifted in from the restaurant dining room.

"Yes, I must talk to Ruby. I must start talking to *all* Dad's friends, especially Matt and the other fisherman on the island. Someone, somewhere must have a clue."

"I think Ruby was waitressing at the Northshore Bait shop when Eldon was last seen there," Clinton said, narrowing his eyes in contemplation. "If Ruby can't help us, I don't know who can. She doesn't miss a trick."

"When did Ruby start working at Northshore?"

"'Bout five months ago after she sold off the Eagle Point tourist cabins and moved into town. When she heard about Eldon, though, she took the rest of the summer off at the bait shop so she could give us a hand. She said to tell you she'll be here tomorrow morning just as soon as she can spring free."

"That's just like Ruby. Always willing to pitch in. By the way, is she still giving piano lessons?" The memory of sitting down to the keyboard with the older woman every Wednesday after school brought a smile to Vanessa's face.

"Nope, she gave that up some time ago. But I swear, she'll never give up her love for all that long-haired music. You know, all that Wolfman Amadeus Mozart stuff. That bull-headed woman's been tryin' to make a convert out of me for ages. "

"You mean *Wolfgang* Amadeus Mozart," she corrected him affectionately.

"Wolfman, Wolfgang, what's the difference?" Clinton asked with a chuckle. "Anyway, I'm sure glad Lowell is here to help. The deck's rotting out, we need more barbecue pits, there are missing boards on the steps to the beach. I could go on and on. Eldon and I were going to tackle those chores together." He pulled a handkerchief from his breast pocket and blew his nose loudly.

"I can help too," she offered quickly. "I'm not too bad with a hammer and nails."

Clinton's mouth twitched. "You mean all your book learnin' didn't change you? You're not afraid of getting your hands fishy-smelling or breaking a fingernail?"

"Of course not."

"Thanks, kiddo, but Lowell and I'll manage." He glanced at the clock on the fireplace mantel. "Ten-thirty already! How about you and I fixin' ourselves a little supper. I'm as hungry as a half-starved grizzly bear, and you must be too."

"I grabbed a bite to eat on the ferry," she answered. "Even then, I wasn't very hungry. As soon as you finish your supper, make sure you get some sleep. You look so tired."

"But the crab pots still need to be hauled in," he protested."

"I already told you. Go to bed. *I'll* haul in the crab pots."

He held up his hands and shook his head in a mock gesture of defeat. "Stubborn, the lady is. Just like her old man."

*****

Inside the sailboat, Lowell sat staring out a porthole. Misty beams of moonlight slanted through. The boat rocked gently, contrasting the turbulence raging within him. He knew it would be hopeless to even try to sleep.

Damn! It was bad enough that Eldon was missing, and now Vanessa was here, complicating the scene. He'd come here to heal, to sort through his life, not wrestle with a *new* batch of problems.

Vanessa. He heaved a sigh, then squared his jaw. He hadn't doubted for a minute she'd come immediately after learning about her father. But he'd dreaded that first meeting. He'd dreaded facing her again. If she only knew he was partly to blame for Eldon's disappearance, she probably would've turned her back on him and asked him to leave. But whatever had happened to that cute little tomboy with braces on her teeth? The one who loved to play tricks and pester him to death?

She's grown up, that's what, his more typical logical side told him. And now what a looker! Sexy from the word go. Did she have any idea how her mane of auburn hair and snapping green eyes could drive a man insane?

He stood up, stretched, and began pacing. Obviously she'd also been caught off guard, though most likely because she hadn't expected to find him there. Apparently Eldon and Clinton hadn't gotten around to telling her, those times she'd phoned, that they'd hired him to help out at the lodge. But then, why should they have? He and Vanessa had never been an item, and sadly enough, Andy was no longer around. Even with the four years separating Andy's birthday from hers, the two of them had been remarkably close.

He stopped pacing and stared at some indiscernible spot on the wall. "Look man," he spoke aloud, his thoughts still riveted on Andy. "I didn't bargain for this. You know what's going on in my life. The last thing I need is a woman messing it up worse. But I won't let you down, man, like I've let down your father. No matter what it takes, I'll do my level best to look out for Vanessa. Make sure that no matter what happens, she somehow gets through this. Yep, that's the least I can do, old buddy.

"For you and *especially* for Eldon."

Chapter Two

After Vanessa unpacked her suitcase and changed into her favorite pair of jeans and a mauve turtleneck sweater, she hurried from her bedroom in the family quarters at the back of the lodge.

Outside, a full moon inched higher in the sky, a gauzy globe of light illuminating the harbor, dock and rocky shoreline. The night was unseasonably balmy for the middle of June, and the moon so bright, she didn't need a flashlight.

As she threaded her way down the pier, a bucket in each hand, she could still feel the warmth of the day beneath her thin-soled sandals. A fish jumped, leaving a widening ripple in the mirror-smooth water.

From the opposite end of the dock, she spotted someone approaching with long-legged strides. A fisherman, no doubt. Except he wasn't carrying any fish, not even a tackle box.

The shadowy figure drew closer. Then she recognized him. Lowell. A jolt coursed through her. Should she pretend she didn't see him and turn back to the lodge?

"What are you doing out here?" he called before she could react. "I thought you were turning in."

She lifted her chin. "Uncle Clint never got around to hauling in the crab pots, and I sent him off to bed. And you? You said you were turning in also."

"I was feeling restless. Thought a walk might help." He gestured to one of the buckets. "I'll take that."

"Thanks. I can handle it."

"But you look exhausted. Seems to me you'd welcome some help."

She shifted beneath his steady gaze. What would it hurt just this once? Besides, he was right—she *was* bone weary.

"Okay. You win." She handed him a bucket and they continued ambling toward the end of the long L-shaped dock where several large crab pots were submerged onto the sea floor.

She caught a whiff of his musky aftershave, noticed the ripple of firm muscles beneath his white polo shirt. Keeping a safe distance between them, she tried to ignore the surge of desire washing over her.

"It would've been a perfect night for sailing," Lowell said, inhaling deeply.

"Yes, the sunset was gorgeous. I saw it as I was getting ready to leave the ferry. If I wasn't so worried about Dad . . . I'd . . . I'd almost feel like a tourist myself."

"I understand."

Beneath the dock floodlights, she stole a glance at his well-chiseled profile, the firm set of his jaw, his easy, wide-swinging gait. She looked up and offered him a tentative smile. "What made you decide to come back home?" she asked. "Why not Alaska? Or the Caribbean perhaps? Seems to me there are plenty of other places where one could run away."

"Roots. Memories." His jaw was set in a grim line. He switched the bucket to his other hand, then added, "Law enforcement has a way of taking its toll. Then one day you finally wake up. You ask yourself whether it's all worthwhile."

"I'm sure you're a terrific cop," she said sincerely. "I'm sure already you've made a positive mark in the world." She adjusted her gait to the subtle rise and fall of the dock. It creaked with each swell of water. Lights from beach homes at the mouth of the bay twinkled.

"Positive mark? That's questionable. Not in the rotten, dog-eat-dog way we live in today. As far as I'm concerned, we've lost all sense of values. No pride. No tradition. No sense of community or family."

"Isn't that a rather harsh slant on life?"

"Depends. Don't forget, your childhood and mine were totally the opposite. I barely knew my dad. Ma worked hard at the cannery to support my three younger brothers and me. She grew old before her time. As you might already know, she ended up in the state hospital a few years ago, then died."

"Yes, I heard. I'm sorry." She fought back the unexpected urge to reach out and hug him.

"Back when we were kids, Ma was always working so many long hours, we rarely saw her." He turned, stopped in his tracks and pinned her with his gaze. "Why do you think I spent so much time hanging out at your place with Andy?"

"I suppose you were lonely. Craving a family."

"Right. I did crave a family. A *real* family. Your folks were plenty busy, too, running the lodge and all, but never too busy to show their warmth and affection. Looking back, I think your father somehow made up for the dad I never knew."

As they started walking again, he lifted his collar against the wind. The simple gesture fascinated her though she couldn't be sure why.

"Yes, Andy and I were never lacking for love," she acknowledged as she sidestepped an open tackle box someone had left on the pier. She hesitated, biting her lip. "Lowell?"

"Yes?"

"I've always been like your little sister. Why can't you tell me what's troubling you?"

"I already explained, Vanessa. I need a break from the grind. I need to get away from police work for a while."

"But there's more. I can tell."

"Don't sweat it. Okay? I'll only be here a short time. It's not worth it to you."

His answer left her with a vague, uneasy feeling. Maybe she *should* leave well enough alone. That was safer for both of them, wasn't it? Right now she suspected they were each battling their own private demons.

At last they came to the end of the dock. Lowell stooped to tug against the rope tied to the first crab pot. Together they began sorting through it. The rustling and clicking of the moving crustaceans sounded like a thousand tiny castanets.

"Were you working here at the lodge when the news came about Dad?" she asked.

"Yep."

"What do you think might have happened?"

"I only wish I knew. Actually, if I hadn't let him down, it's possible all this might've never happened."

"What are you talking about?"

"Everyone's saying that Matt should've gone with him the morning he left, but that's not entirely true. I was the one who was supposed to go. Your father and I had planned to check out some fishing sites near the North Spit, then spend the rest of the day trawling. But first he wanted to stop by the bait shop to gas up, buy his usual six-pack, and chew the fat for a little while with the locals." He swallowed hard before continuing. "For some crazy reason my alarm never went off. I'm not sure why Eldon didn't come down to the dock to wake me. He probably figured I needed my rest since I'd been up late the night before tearing out old Sheetrock." Jerking his gaze from hers, he added, "I dreaded seeing you again, Vanessa. I dreaded telling you that. I haven't even told Clinton yet."

The silence loomed between them. "Well, I see," she said at last.

"You're angry. I can tell."

She shook her head, biting back tears. "No. Not angry. *Frightened.* I'm scared out of my wits, Lowell. I can't bear the thought of losing Dad. Dad's all I've got left anymore, besides Uncle Clint." *And if I fall in love with you, something terrible might happen to you too.*

He looked back at her. His lips parted as if he was about to say something, yet he remained silent.

"If I should be angry with anyone, perhaps it should be Dad," she continued. "He knew better than to go out alone. I can only pray now that Dad is alive and unharmed and will come back home soon."

"Yes, that's all any of us can hope for."

As they continued tossing the legal-sized crabs into a bucket, their hands touched. Instinctively she drew hers away. So many times back in high school had she longed to be near him like this. Just Lowell and herself, without Andy anywhere around. Again the rush of memories surfaced, like a skin diver plunging back from the depths of the sea.

She groped for small-talk. "I bet Kaloch Bay grows some of the most delicious Dungeness crabs in the entire Pacific Northwest. Hopefully, there'll be plenty here to make up a big batch of my famous Crab Supreme."

He chuckled, the sound punctuating the still night. "I remember. I can still see it now. The first time you tried out your culinary efforts on Andy and me, I swear we ended up spitting out more pieces of shells than eating."

Her hand flew to her mouth as she repressed her own chuckle. "Don't remind me. But I do believe Dad told you and Andy to clean them. We all had equal stake in that little fiasco."

"Andy. Man, how I miss him."

The longing in his voice twisted her heart. She stared hard into the darkness. "Yeah, I know. Me too."

"If Andy were still alive," he went on, "I bet we'd be together on this dock right now hauling in the crab pots. Just like we used to. We'd also be swapping stories, maybe a private joke or two."

And I'd still be Andy's little sis, she thought. *Nothing but a tag-along.* Guilt flooded over her. God only knew, she'd give almost anything to have her brother back.

He hefted up the next crab pot and they sorted through the last of their catch.

"Where's your brother's boat?" Vanessa asked as she scanned the next section of dock past several white sails and thick mastheads.

"Last one on the dock." He pointed. "Sea Breeze.

"Wow!" she exclaimed, her mouth dropping open. The sailboat's bowsprit jetted forth majestically, its polished wooden door that led inside the cabin caught glimmers of moonlight.

"Like to take a quick tour?" He darted her an uncertain look.

"Well, just for a few minutes. It's getting late."

Inside, Lowell grinned, then spread his hands wide. "And this, my fair maid, is the ballroom galley. The dance begins at nine o'clock sharp."

His sudden light-heartedness was unexpectedly endearing.

"In case you haven't noticed, it's almost midnight," she teased back. "Guess we missed out."

He flicked on a small brass lamp mounted to the wall. "Would you care for a glass of wine?"

"I really don't have time for that."

"It'll help you sleep."

She hesitated, knowing it had been a mistake to step inside in the first place. Lowell's magnetic nearness, the small galley, the moonlight shimmering across the water—it was much too intimate, yet she yearned for just a few moments more.

"All right," she answered. "But like I just said a minute ago, I can't stay long." She slipped into a small booth and accepted the glass of wine. He sat down across from her, his own glass in hand.

Without warning, a shrill bark cut through the stillness. She looked up and spied a shaggy gray terrier bounding onto her lap. The dog covered her face with warm, wet licks.

She convulsed in laughter. "Oh, what a darling dog! And what a greeting?"

"That's Toby. My pride and joy. The thought of boarding him in a kennel while I was away didn't quite set right, so I brought him with me." His smile lingered affectionately on the dog, who'd promptly curled upon Vanessa's lap. "So what do you think?" he asked, pausing to take a sip of wine. "About my brother's boat, I mean?"

"It's beautiful both inside and out."

"When Sam and I were kids, we always dream of owning a sailboat someday. Of course, there was no money for it then. And our other two brothers, John and Jeremy, were more interested in motorcycles than boats."

"Ah, yes. The twins, John and Jeremy. Where are they now?" Absently she stroked the dog's silky fur.

"They've both moved to Montana. Plenty of open country there where they can ride their bikes to their hearts' content."

"So you were the only one who didn't end up with a grown-up toy . . ."

"Right. No time. Too busy tracking down the bad guys, I guess." One corner of his mouth lifted in a wry smile.

Unexpectedly a thought popped into her head. A thought that left her nearly breathless and charged with energy. What she needed now was a cop. A cop to help in her own private search for her father. A cop just like Lowell. So what if he seemed preoccupied with the dark side of life? Maybe that's what it took. Someone who wasn't afraid to get his hands dirty. Someone with an inquiring mind . . .

All she had to do now was ask.

*****

"Look for Eldon? You think <u>I</u> can help?" Lowell darted her a skeptical look as they strolled back down the dock to retrieve the crab pots.

"Of course. And as far as I'm concerned, the sooner we get started, the better."

"The Coast Guard is out in full force. The choppers and rescue vessels are covering more ground than you and I could ever begin to."

"But what's to say we can't look too? I *know* we can make a difference. I'll simply go crazy if I don't somehow get involved." The moon had inched higher, half hidden behind a wispy layer of dark clouds.

"I'm not sure how I can spring free," Lowell answered evenly. "Clinton needs me more than ever now." He turned to her. In the wash of moonlight, his face was lined with painful indecision.

He's holding back. What I'm asking is too much like police work—the very thing he says he needs a break from. But I'm only here for a very short while. I need his help.

"Please, Lowell," she urged gently. "I'll talk to Clinton. I'm sure he'll understand."

"Give me some time. I may not be able to help you tomorrow, but that's not saying I can't later. I really want to. Believe me."

She sighed deeply. "All right then. I'll go by myself."

"Be careful, Vanessa." His eyes bore into hers.

"I will."

As they came to the end of the dock and crossed the narrow strip of beach, a shudder raced through her. Was it because of the advancing chill of marine night air, her anxious feelings about her father, or the reality of how she and Lowell had been so unexpectedly thrust together again? In less than twenty-four hours, it seemed, her life had accelerated nearly out of control. Why, just last night she'd been back home, warm and snug, enjoying a quiet reprieve from her usual busy schedule.

Her support group took up three evenings a week. By devoting herself to helping others, it left little time for the opposite sex—and that's the way she liked it. How could she ever love again when two of the people most dear to her had been so suddenly whisked out of her life? And now with Eldon's fate in question, she felt even more vulnerable.

What was more, the kids needed her. Already in just a few weeks, they were beginning to shed their defenses and open up not only with her, but also with each other. Especially Carmen, the petite dark-haired fifteen-year-old who'd appeared the most withdrawn in the beginning. Then last night came that fateful call from Clinton with all that had followed. And now Lowell. Goodness only knew, it was difficult enough trying to help Clinton run the lodge, deal with the search and rescue officials, the local sheriff's department, and the news media plus get on with her own search. Lowell's virile male presence was definitely a complication. She wasn't prepared to deal with her perplexing feelings for him.

At last, they arrived at the back door of the family quarters, next to a trellis laden with scarlet roses.

The shadows muted the sharp angels of his face as she heard him laugh. "This is crazy, isn't it?" he said. "We already said good-night a few hours ago."

She laughed too. "Yes, I guess we did."

He snapped off a rose, then twirled it in his fingers, staring down at it. "You leaving first thing tomorrow?"

"I'd like to, but I'll have to wait till Ruby arrives first. She's offered to help run the office."

"So what's your agenda?" he asked. "Where are you planning to start?"

"Most likely I'll drive first to the North Spit to watch the Coast Guard efforts. If one of the copters or rescue boats finds him, I want to be right there. I want to be the first one to welcome him home."

"And if they don't find him?"

"Then I'll come back here. I'll fire up one of the motorboats and head over to the peninsula across from the North Spit."

His eyes flitted down to her lips, then back up. "You are one determined lady, aren't you?"

"What choice have I?"

He nodded in silent understanding. "You'd better not waste any time getting these crabs in the coolers."

"I won't. Good night again, Lowell."

"'Night, Vanessa."

Moments later after she'd slipped inside, she parted the curtains and stole another look through the misty moon light to the dock below. Lowell was standing next to his sailboat gazing up at the lodge.

*****

Next morning after phoning Matt at the Eagle Point cabins and learning he'd left to go fishing, Vanessa searched feverishly through the file cabinets in the office. Hopefully Ruby would arrive soon. Clinton hadn't indicated an exact time, if in fact, she had mentioned one. But at least this would give Vanessa a chance to do a bit of detective work before she left to watch the search and rescue efforts, she decided. The first folder bulged with old receipts. Did Dad have any outstanding debts that could have somehow triggered his disappearance? Had creditors issued a warning? Perhaps some disgruntled guest had harbored a grudge and plotted against him. She must also remember to peruse the lodge guest book. Maybe there'd be some thinly veiled clue in the *comments* column, one that had somehow gone overlooked.

"Mornin', Miss Paris."

She looked up from the file cabinet and saw Lawrence Wallace, the grandfatherly gardener, smiling down at her. His large bulky frame nearly filled the doorway.

"Good morning, Lawrence. Oh, by the way, someone called earlier this morning from the wholesale nursery in town. A Mr. Peterson, I believe. He said the flats of petunias you ordered are ready to go."

"Finally," the man said with a pleased look. "I was beginning to think we'd have to fill the flower beds this year with something else. Seems there's been an unusal demand for petunias, especially the white fragrant ones that your father loves so."

"Yes, Dad's favorite." Her heart twisted.

Outside she could hear the drone of a copter, mingled with the sounds of Lowell hammering and sawing on the back deck. Vanessa pushed back the uneasy feelings the reminder of him evoked within her.

Why couldn't he have opted to work for one of the other lodge owners instead right now? There were at least a dozen on the island. Given the ever-constant reality of Lowell's presence, it was going to be harder than ever to wipe him out of her mind.

Lawrence fished a crumpled Kleenex from the pocket of his overalls and blew his nose loudly. "Poor Eldon, I do hope we hear something soon. God bless him. Why, he's the last person I ever thought would end up missing."

"Yes, the waiting is pure agony," Vanessa agreed, her emotions wavering between raw determination and cold, hard fear. I don't know how any of us can keep going on this way."

"Now don't you worry about nothin', Miss Paris," Lawrence said, patting her shoulder. "I'll keep everything ship shape as far as the grounds-keeping goes. I know you got plenty on your mind without worrying about that too." He started back out the door. "And for now, it's high time I got to work. Be sure and let me know the minute you hear anything."

Vanessa attempted a smile. "Thanks, Lawrence. I will."

She wandered over to the map of the San Juan Islands tacked on the wood-paneled wall opposite the file cabinet. Chewing her lower lip in concentration, she focused on the peninsula where she intended to search. It was an elongated finger of land, stretching for several miles from east to west with no electricity, no roadways, not even a handful of small summer cabins. A narrow channel separated it from the North Spit.

Despite Dad's heart condition, he was a strong swimmer and well-versed in survival skills, she reminded herself. If he was swept off his boat in the channel, chances were good he might have swum to the peninsula. Granted, the Sound remained icy cold all year round, but the passageway was narrow enough to permit this small miracle.

Perhaps he'd camped out on the long stretch of beach or farther back in the scraggly growth of trees that bordered it. The Coast Guard must've simply missed sight of his campfire yesterday. Or the SOS signals he'd undoubtedly flashed into the darkening sky last night.

She looked up as Clinton entered the office. He was wearing a green wool shirt, baggy trousers, and black high-top rubber boots, typical dress of the island locals. "Oh, you're here," she greeted him. "I thought you left at the crack of dawn with the group trawling for salmon."

"That's on for tomorrow. Today I'm taking some folks clam diggin'. Low tide's at ten. They didn't come outfitted with buckets, boots and the right shovels—funny how unprepared these city-slickers usually are, so I said I'd take care of everything." He tapped his pipe against the counter, then continued, "Anyway, I hear the clamming's best near Johnson's landing, so we'll head over there first."

His glance fell onto her stack of past receipts. "So what's up, kiddo? Don't the books balance? Are we behind in our payments?"

Neither her father or uncle were interested in keeping their records on a computer, so they'd just relied on old-fashioned bookkeeping.

"Everything's fine. I'm just tidying up, that's all. I was also hoping these old receipts might somehow turn up a clue about Dad, but so far, nothing."

He listened intently while she briefed him in on her plans. "I wonder what's taking Ruby so long?" she added, glancing at the clock on the wall. "It's already past nine. I hope she hasn't forgotten."

The corner of his mouth lifted slightly. "Don't worry. That woman never forgets nothin'." He sent Vanessa an apologetic look. "Wish I could go with you, but I can't let the lodge guests down. Tough as it is, I'll just have to keep telling myself it's business as usual. We've been askin' folks to pay up for the excursions in advance. We'd lose our good reputation if word got out that we didn't keep our promises."

"Of course, Uncle Clint. I realize that."

"Any luck getting in touch with Matt?"

"I'm afraid not. I've called him on his cell phone a couple of times and tried his landline at the cabins. The answering machine said everyone had already left for another guided fishing excursion."

The sounds of Lowell's hammering had stopped, and Vanessa couldn't help hoping he might saunter into the office to announce he'd changed his mind and had decided to go with her after all.

He didn't.

Clinton polished his eyeglasses with the corner of his shirt tail, then slipped them back on. "If you do manage to catch up with Matt later, tell him to stop by. I want to get his opinion of the new rod and reel I picked up last week."

"I will." Their conversation about Ruby and Matt brought an unexpected question to her mind. "Uncle Clint . . . "

"Yes, kiddo?"

"Whatever made Ruby decide to lease her property?" Vanessa knew that the older woman had been contemplating the change but never suspected she'd follow through. The cabins and surrounding thirty acres of prime Douglas fir had been in Ruby's family for nearly a century and a half.

"Work just got too much for her. Even though Matt's been her right-hand man ever since her hubby died, she said she woke up one day and told herself, enough was enough. What she was hankerin' for instead was a nice little part-time job in town without the long hours and responsibility." He ran his large-boned hands across a light stubble of beard and stared absently outside the window.

"Too bad Matt didn't decide to retire also," Vanessa said. "I expect by now he's long over-due for a rest too."

"That's why your pop's been complainin' that Matt can never go fishin' with him anymore. He seems to think the new managers, Josh Buckler and his cousin Dolly can't get along without him."

"I hope they're paying Matt well. He deserves it."

"I hope so too. Ever since Fern, his wife, had that stroke last year and he had to put her in a nursin' home, he's been scrapin' by to make ends meet." He frowned. "I hear the Bucklers are real green-horns when it comes to tourists and no doubt need someone like Matt. I still wish, though, he would've come to work for Eldon and me instead."

An image of her father swam up in her mind and again she fought back tears. Stocky, barrel-chested, he stood barely five-and-a-half feet, a sharp contrast to her tall, lanky uncle. Though Dad's blue eyes often laughed from beneath bushy brows, they also held a distant, gray look whenever he was troubled.

The reasons were obvious, she reminded herself. The past few years had taken its toll on both of them. Yet through it all, she and Dad had grown even closer. His love for her had always sustained her.

"You can do it, kitten," he used to say. "My little girl will always come out on top." Remembering, more tears threatened. She felt a dull ache in the pit of her stomach, a lump forming at the base of her throat.

The slam of the office door intruded on Vanessa's thoughts. With a start, she looked up and saw Ruby. Rushing to meet her, Vanessa flung her arms around the older woman's bird-like frame. "Oh, Ruby! Thanks for coming. You'll never know how much this means." Blinking back tears, Vanessa inhaled the scent of Ruby's honeysuckle cologne, felt the warmth of her answering embrace. Mama might no longer be here, but at least Ruby was.

"Anything to help, child," Ruby replied brokenly. "Anything at all."

Chapter Three

Vanessa steered her black Mazda down the asphalt two-lane road that snaked its way along the east shoreline of Tawanya Island. Though all her friends from school days had long since left, few of the old landmarks had changed. The same ramshackle mom-pop store she'd just driven by, the same sprawling church campgrounds in plain view ahead. Yet the vague uneasiness gnawing at her was growing worse by the hour. If something terrible had happened to Dad, the comfortable familiarity could suddenly disappear forever.

But no! She gave a quick shake of her head. Something terrible had *not* happened! Dad had taught her to look at the bright side of life—despite all their misfortune. He was alive. She just knew it. Alive and waiting for her. And she'd do everything in her power to prove it.

Turning right, she hurried past fields of grazing cattle and profuse explosions of wild roses. She could hear the drone of another helicopter, or perhaps it was one of the two she'd already spotted earlier that morning.

More memories from childhood wrapped around her. Her father was tough and grizzled, a testament to his former years as an independent commercial fisherman. But carving out a livelihood on the sea had been rough, the income unpredictable and so her parents had decided to purchase the guest lodge when Vanessa was less than two.

Still, the call of the sea beckoned Eldon, a call so compelling he couldn't turn his back. That's when he started up his own fishing guide service and Uncle Clinton had moved in to take on joint ownership. After all, the other guide services on the island could stand a little friendly competition, Dad had always announced with a good-natured chuckle.

The rumble of an approaching school bus from the church camp jarred her from her reminiscence. Glancing off to the side, she caught sight of two Coast Guard cutters cruising up the Sound. Her pulse raced with anticipation. They appeared to be heading in the direction of the copter which was now hovering above a rocky cliff beyond.

She turned onto the next road that led to the beach, then skidded to a stop in the narrow parking strip above it. A group of bicyclists wearing helmets and black riding garb were clustered nearby, watching the search efforts. Other locals had gathered as well.

Vanessa grabbed her binoculars from beneath the driver's seat, then flung open the car door and picked her way down the sandy trail that was fringed by wild beach grass. Thank goodness, the on-lookers were absorbed in the search efforts, and she managed to slip by them unnoticed. Coming to the uppermost portion of beach, her sandaled feet sunk into the dry soft sand. The warmth penetrated her feet, contrasting with the cool mid-morning breeze that fanned her flushed cheeks. The skies were clear, perfect visibility for the search and rescue crews.

At last she came to the cooler, compact ribbon of beach closer to the water's edge. She stopped, shading her eyes and again turned her attention towards the copter. It was fluttering above the rocky promontory like a great silver hummingbird. Suddenly the helicopter lifted, its blades chopping the air as it turned southward, then disappeared out of sight.

A sinking feeling settled in the pit of her stomach. She turned her gaze to the expanse of beach, the sea, the sky. "If only I could've been here when he left," she cried aloud. "Maybe I could've stopped him." A surge of tears welled up in her eyes, a sob caught in the back of her throat.

"No. If anyone should've stopped him, it was me, not you."

She spun around and spotted Lowell gazing down at her. Where had he come from? How long had he been following her? She'd never even heard footsteps.

"Lowell! I didn't think anyone else was here. Especially not you," she blurted.

He cupped his hand on her shoulder and his warm, strong grip seemed to sear through her. His piercing blue eyes appeared nearly as blue as the water itself as his gaze held hers. "I was on my way to pick up the new order of lumber. I noticed your car, and saw you take the turn off to the beach."

"But why? Why did you decide to follow me?"

"All morning I've been arguing with myself, knowing I had to talk to you. When I spotted you driving in front of me, I knew I couldn't put it off a minute longer."

"Put off talking to me? About what?"

His gaze held hers. "I'm going with you, Vanessa. I can't let you do this alone."

*****

"Off at last," Vanessa said to Lowell as she maneuvered the motor boat away from the dock. She was still numb with disbelief. He'd agreed to help her. At least for this one day.

"I hope the weather cooperates," he said, casting a wary look at the sky. "The forecaster on the morning news predicted showers." He was sitting next to her, dressed in a pale blue tank top and light tan walking shorts. Every now and then, his shoulder brushed hers, sending tremors of excitement down her spine. How was she going to keep focused on looking for her father when Lowell's very presence was causing her heart to beat in double time?

The wind lifted her hair as they entered the mouth of the bay. White-tipped waves rippled the Sound.

"You remembered to bring your rain slicker, I hope," he commented matter-of-factly.

She gave him a mock salute. "Aye, aye captain! Right in my gym bag. What about you?"

"Yep. Prepared as always. Rain gear. N'orwester hat." He nodded to the khaki green pack he'd stuffed beneath the rear seat. My years as a Boy Scout paid off after all. I even have the merit badges to prove it."

"Listen to you," she teased. "A big tough L.A. cop bragging about Boy Scout badges."

The light-hearted exchange felt wonderful, she told herself as they puttered past a commercial fishing boat. She needed this fleeting reprieve. The stress of the past couple of days was frazzling her nerves. And Lowell's heart-stopping grin—ah, shades of years past.

Sighing, she pictured the look on his face the time he discovered she'd slathered the inside of his sleeping bag with shaving cream while he and Andy were getting ready for a weekend camping trip with the Eagle Scouts. And the night he'd stopped by for a barbecue with her family and she'd stuck fake plastic ice cubes into his lemonade glass, the kind of fake ice cubes that contained equally fake ants in the middle.

In both instances, Lowell had playfully threatened to throttle her, and she'd been beside herself with happiness. At last, if only for a moment, she'd managed to capture his attention. Quickly she pushed away the memories. The important thing now was the search.

"Take my binoculars," she said. "They're right below your seat. See if you can spot any distress signals on a beach, or maybe smoke from a campfire."

He did as she'd said, scanning the horizon, while she concentrated on navigating the boat.

"See anything?" she asked.

"No. Nothing out of the ordinary."

Turning the boat into the wind, they continued north. A fine spray misted her sunglasses. he licked her lips, catching a hint of saltiness. On the shoreline, red-barked madronas glistened while farther inland, groves of Douglas fir intermingled with birch and cedar. Straight ahead clusters of smaller islands dotted the inlet like sun-washed emeralds.

"So what are your plans after we come to the peninsula?" Lowell asked, resting the binoculars on his lap.

"We can tie up near the tide flats," she answered. "Then we'll head back to that stretch of forest inland. If Dad was trying to find shelter, I suspect it would've been there. He used to go bear hunting in those woods, but ever since he decided to get involved with conservation efforts a year or two ago, he turned in his rifle for a camera."

Lowell nodded. "I'm well acquainted with that part of the peninsula too. Andy and I used to go clam digging over there on that short stretch of beach. Man, did we ever have some great times."

"You did? You crossed the channel alone?" Alarm filled her.

"Yep."

"But the channel was off-limits. My folks always warned us, you too, about strong currents."

One corner of his mouth turned up. "Our families never had a clue, we made sure of that. We also liked to climb the girders at Moser's Bridge and see how far we could dare each other to edge out over the water."

"No! You must be kidding!"

"'Fraid not."

She darted him a look. "Poor Mama. Perhaps it's good she didn't know. If she'd suspected even half of what you two were doing, she'd have been nuts with worry. Your mother too."

"Don't think we didn't realize that," he answered. "But as the old saying goes, boys will be boys, and I guess our search for adventure outweighed common sense. Now when I look back, I know I wouldn't want any kid of mine to pull the stunts I used to." He shook his head and added, "God knows, my mother certainly didn't need any more worries than she already had."

"Why do you suppose your parents didn't stay together?"

"Most likely it was because they were married much too young. Barely out of high school. I suppose my father wasn't ready for the responsibility of raising a family. At any rate, we never heard from him again after he split." A frown puckered Lowell's mouth. "He might as well have been dead as far as we were concerned."

"Oh no! How can you say that?"

"It's true. He never phoned. He never came back for a visit. Not even a birthday card or an email for any of us."

She bit her lip, glancing down at the depth-finder. No wonder he'd taken to her father so that year before he'd left the island.

At the thought of Eldon, a pang shot through her. *Dad, where are you? You've got to be somewhere. You've got to be alive.* Today marked the second full day since his disappearance. How long could he stay well without his heart medicine?

Lowell must've sensed her thoughts. "How many pills was Eldon taking?"

"One on a daily basis," she answered, steering the boat into deeper waters to avoid an underlying reef. "A Digitoxin pill to help control his erratic heartbeat. The other, his Nitro, for whenever he's having chest pain."

Lowell's expression was sober. "I know all about the Nitro. These past few weeks he's needed it several times."

"*Several times?*" Were her ears deceiving her?

"That's right."

"Are you sure?"

"Absolutely."

Her spirits sank. "Did Dad tell his doctor about this?"

"I doubt it. You know Eldon. It was always hard to get him to go to a doctor in the first place. Besides, he never wanted anyone to fuss over him."

"So true." She exhaled slowly. "Was Dad under a lot of stress lately, Lowell? Was he working harder than he should've been?"

"Not that I was aware of, although I have to admit, I may have missed any signs."

The peninsula was in plain view now. The narrow beach shimmered in the afternoon sun while the cliffs and forest beyond stretched out like the spiny back of a giant alligator.

"Maybe those episodes were really nothing," she mused out loud. "I mean, maybe it was simply some indigestion or a pulled muscle."

"Hmm." He looked doubtful.

"We can't dismiss that possibility," she pointed out. Overhead a seagull screeched while it drifted on a current of air. "Dad used to have an ulcer, you know. There's nothing saying it couldn't have come back."

"No, I suppose not. But just make sure you're not denying the obvious, Vanessa. Heart disease is nothing to mess around with."

She stiffened. "I'm a psychologist, remember. I know all about denial. If you're insinuating—"

"I'm only reporting the facts as I witnessed them," he interrupted her. "Your father's episodes of chest pain were occurring about once every week. That figures on the average of four times a month. Those odds aren't good. Not good at all."

Drawing in a steadying breath, she looked the other way. *Reports. Facts. Statistics.* Just like a cop. He might think she was in denial, but that simply wasn't true. No one realized more fully the ups and downs of Eldon's life, especially now that her mother and Andy were gone. How could she be so attracted to a man who was so incompatible with her? One thing she knew for certain. She wasn't ready to deal with his cold, hard world.

One hour merged into the next. By early evening they'd turned back. So far they'd found nothing.

"When we get back to the North Spit," Vanessa said, "let's talk with the officers at the Coast Guard station. See whether they've learned anything while we've been away."

"I was just about ready to suggest that myself. Clinton said the Coast Guard would maintain their search efforts till dark, but surely the officers back at the station will know something."

Later, after tying up at the public dock, they trekked down the ribbon of beach that led to the Coast Guard Station. It'd been a long, exhausting day. She was tired of thinking about where to look next. Tired of speculating what might've happened to her father. Somehow, too, her thoughts kept swinging back to Lowell's proclamation late last night. Police *work has a way of taking its toll.* Whatever had prompted his need to flee back to the islands, it was apparent he'd been affected by it greatly. Once again the possibilities paraded through her mind.

"Lowell." She stopped in her tracks and turned to face him. The wind was tousling his sandy blond hair. He looked so alive. So incredibly handsome.

"Yes?"

She drew in a breath, posing the question that had been plaguing her ever since they'd met again. "You've been married, haven't you? Your work on the police force interfered with your marriage."

He gave a quick, derisive laugh. "There you go again. Worrying about me. I'm not one of your clients, and you're certainly not my shrink. Most of all, I'm not here to focus on relationships—professional or otherwise. But I will say this much. You're wrong about the marriage bit. I've always been single."

"I'm sorry. I didn't mean to over-step my boundaries."

His eyes were forgiving as he flashed her a grin. "You always were a snoopy little thing, weren't you? Andy used to complain how you'd sometimes listen in on his phone calls."

"So?" she taunted him. "Isn't that what little sisters are supposed to do?" She couldn't ignore the powerful force drawing her to him, the attraction that was spiraling nearly out-of-control.

"I don't know. I never had one." This time his look remained closed.

As they strode on, Lowell took her hand in his. Confusion swept over her. What did it mean to Lowell, this physical contact? His large hand clasped around hers felt protective, commanding and not entirely just a brotherly gesture.

The sun, a fiery red ball, was sinking below the west horizon. In the last slanting rays, the beach and sky were washed in a rose-sherbet glow.

Pausing momentarily, they studied a crystalline tidal pool, commenting on its beauty. On the outer rim of rocks, tight clusters of dark-blue and white mussels clung with glue like tenacity. Inside, a rust-colored hermit crab skittered beneath a cluster of green flowered sea anemones.

Yet the peacefulness surrounding them seemed to make a mockery of Vanessa's churning thoughts. Not only was Lowell's enigmatic behavior weighing heavy on her mind, but their afternoon on the peninsula had been exhausting. After crossing the tidelands, they'd hiked through the forest for nearly six miles. And all the while, she couldn't forget Lowell's news about her father's angina attacks. What if Dad was in serious trouble right now? *What if he'd never left the "Lady Luck" alive in the first place?*

With a start, she pushed the frightening thought to the farthest recesses of her mind. No, she had to hold her head high. Her father would be disappointed in her if she gave up so soon.

Stepping over a gnarled piece of driftwood, she inhaled deeply of the invigorating salt air and felt her tension momentarily drain away. "I can't blame you for coming back here, Lowell. Each time I'm away, I tend to forget how healing it is."

"Me too." His voice trailed as he let go of her hand and held her gaze. "Now it's my turn to ask questions. What about *your* love life? Any romantic ghosts for you? Fair's fair, you know."

"I'm much too busy for romance. And I prefer it that way."

"Oh?" The surprise in his voice came through loud and clear.

"Falling in love requires too much. I'm not willing to pay the price."

He stopped walking and tipped her chin up with his hand, facing her squarely. "You speak from past experience?"

She could only lift one shoulder in a half-hearted shrug.

"What kind of answer is that? Especially after you accused *me* of being evasive?"

"Well," she paused, "of course there have been a few men."

"Not surprising." His eyes roved over her appreciatively.

"But nothing ever came of my relationships with them," she was quick to point out. "They've remained only friends. Some were willing to go along with that and stick around on my terms. The others who wanted more . . . well," she shrugged again, "they simply moved on to greener pastures."

"You mean you never wanted a permanent commitment?"

"No."

"Why not?"

"If I were to fall in love, perhaps even marry, I'd only put myself in jeopardy. My husband might die. Just like Mom and Andy did, and now maybe Dad."

His face darkened. "That may be true, but you're much too young and pretty. Don't hide yourself away forever, Vanessa."

"Far better a contented spinster, than a heart-broken widow."

"I can't believe you really mean that."

"Well, believe it. I've never meant anything more." Overhead a seagull shrieked, then swooped down onto the sand.

"Look." He pursed his lips, as if considering how to go on. "I'm going to give you some brotherly advice, just like Andy would do if he were here right now."

"I thought you didn't want to talk about relationships," she reminded him tersely.

"This is different. This time we're talking about you."

"So there's a double standard? What applies to you doesn't apply to me?"

"I'm sorry. I'm just trying to look out for you. Andy would expect that much of me. I *know* he would."

She ignored the sting of truth underscoring his words. "I can't argue that Andy would want you to help me look for Dad. After all, I was the one who first suggested that. But I know Andy wouldn't want you to try to run my life. Leave that up to me, Lowell. I'm a big girl now."

"Fair enough. I don't need a therapist and you don't need a big brother. Right?"

"Exactly."

He let out a slow, shaky breath. "So on to other things, like where are you living on the mainland? Where do you call home?"

Her stomach was still turning somersaults, but she willed her voice to sound casual. "I rent a condo in Edmonds, about a fifteen-minute drive north of the university. Edmonds is a lovely little town with several restaurants overlooking the beach, a ferry that goes to Kingston, and lots of quaint gift shops and boutiques."

"Yes, I drove through there once." He hesitated. "So how long can you stay this summer? When must you go back?"

"I'm afraid I'm here on limited time, just like you. I told my colleagues at the university I'll return in about four weeks. I must get back to my teen support group too. The kids are depending on me." She paused as two joggers in grey sweats passed by.

"Have you talked to Ruby yet?" he asked. The summer before his senior year in high school, Lowell had worked for Ruby's husband, doing odd jobs at the cabins. He'd grown fond of the older couple, as had practically everyone else who had also known them.

"I've only talked with her briefly. We plan to visit more as soon as I get back tonight. I told Clinton to make sure she stays till I get there." A smile lifted Vanessa's lip. "And I'm sure she'll take every opportunity to do just that. It sounds as if she hasn't given up on my uncle and whether he realizes it or not, he's eventually going to come around."

"Ah ha!" Lowell gave a deep-throated chuckle. "Maybe I should warn Clinton before it's too late and he finds himself in the clutches of this scheming female."

"Don't you dare! Ruby would be perfect for him, whether she's scheming or—" She broke off suddenly, pointing about fifteen feet out into the water. "Look! Sea otters! Maybe a dozen or more. It's been ages since I've seen so many."

"Technically they're river otters," he explained. "In spite of their name, the river otters here in the islands have adapted to salt water quite well. True sea otters are usually spotted farther out past the Straits of Juan De Fuca towards the ocean."

The piercing sound of the air station siren sliced through their conversation.

Vanessa jerked her attention toward the take-off strip where three men were running to a waiting helicopter. In seconds, light flashing, blades pulsating, it ascended, turned sharply, and disappeared over a jagged edge of dark trees.

Chapter Four

Vanessa gripped Lowell's arm and exclaimed, "The siren! What does it mean? Something about Dad?"

"I doubt it." He turned to her, his eyes two deep blue pools. "I doubt if very much. If an alert had come through, they probably would've dispatched one of the copters already in flight. It's not quite dark yet, so I assume they're still out there looking."

Adrenaline coursed through her. No, she wouldn't accept his answer. He had to be wrong! She darted a glance at the sweep of beach fronting the air center and spotted three uniformed men. They were peering up at the sky.

"But we've got to find out," she insisted. "This might be what we've been waiting for!" She pointed at the men. "Maybe those officers can tell us something."

"Vanessa." He planted both hands on her shoulders. His touch was dangerous. "Didn't you hear me? I doubt if that call had anything to do with Eldon."

Pulling away, she charged down the beach, waving her hands and hollering. The men were staring back at her with obvious concern. About midway in the channel, a tug boat pulled a barge.

"Hey lady," one of the men shouted the minute she was within ear-shot. "What's the matter? That guy on the beach. Is he giving you a bad time?"

"No! No!" she puffed, breaking her stride. "That's just Lowell. He's . . . he's . . . a friend." She felt her face grow hot with embarrassment. "I'm Eldon Paris's daughter. He's the fisherman you've been looking for. Have you heard news about him?"

"Sorry, ma'am," the second Coast Guardsman answered. "The communication station called in the alert. There's a commercial fishing boat in trouble across the channel. As far as I know, we still have no word about your father."

"But are you sure?"

"Absolutely. The radioman confirmed it a few minutes ago before we ended our shift."

A crow cawed raucously as it winged its way beyond the flight tower. The sky had darkened, bringing a blanket of grey clouds, and raindrops pattered against the already damp sand.

"Yes, of course." Hot tears mingled with the rain, blinding her eyes. Numb with disappointment, she turned and started back. Lowell was sprinting up the beach to catch up to her.

"There's no point going any farther," she told him after she'd closed the distance between them. "I already found out."

"Still no word, huh?"

"No, I'm afraid not." The tears spilled down her cheeks.

"Ah, Nessie. Don't cry. Please don't." He gathered her to him and planted a soft kiss on the top of her head. He resisted the urge to say I told you so while at the same time he ached to hold her tight.

At the sound of her nick-name, she blinked back more tears. She couldn't remember Lowell ever calling her that before. Only Andy, Mama, and Dad had. "It's no use," she sobbed. "We'll never see Dad again."

"Don't say that."

"Well, it's true. He's dead! I just know it. All the talk about what a great fisherman he was. Little good it must've done him in the end."

Throwing caution aside, he embraced her, pressing her face against his chest. She felt so small and scared—and somehow so right in his arms.

What am I doing? he silently demanded. How did I let this happen? But what self-respecting guy could stand by and just allow her to cry? God, how he hated to see a woman cry.

She yearned to lose herself in his comforting strength, the warm assurance of his masculine nearness. Unthinkingly, she reached up to twine her fingers through his hair, then stopped instantly. No, she couldn't allow herself more than this fleeting moment, this one quick embrace. They were simply two human beings sharing a mutual concern, the disappearance of her father.

"Nessie, listen to me." He brushed back a stray lock of hair from her forehead. "Don't pack it in yet. It's much too early. Besides, this isn't like you. What happened to your positive outlook? Your refusal to give up?"

"I haven't given up, it's just that sometimes it's so hard. I'm only human, don't forget."

His mouth brushed her cheek. "I understand."

His tenderness temporarily disarmed her. She needed his comfort. She needed his strong, masculine arms around her. But he was only her big brother's buddy. A tantalizingly good-looking cop with a much too logical mind, and an apparent dark problem he'd only partially revealed.

"I really do admire your optimism," he went on, "even if it may seem I don't always agree. Don't ever lose it. It's something a few cops like me could learn a lesson from."

She swiped at a tear with the back of her hand, then pulled away. "Do you really mean that?"

"I've never meant anything more." Gently lifting her chin with his thumb, he gazed into her eyes. His expression was filled with an intensity that nearly robbed her of her breath.

"Lowell."

"Shh! Not now . . ." His lips pressed down against hers, silencing her next words. Linking her arms around his neck, she leaned into him, kissing him back. His kiss felt warm and urgent, even more incredible than she'd dared to dream. She opened her mouth and his tongue explored hers—tasting, tempting, and hopelessly intoxicating.

The kiss deepened. It might have lasted a minute, an hour, an eternity, perhaps before they finally broke the contact and strolled arm-in-arm back down the beach. Yet one thing she did know for sure, she'd just glimpsed Paradise.

And it could never be hers.

*****

Lowell stacked the last 2x4 on the end of the deck. There! All ready for him to get back to work. That's what he needed to get his head on straight. Plain old-fashioned work and plenty of it. Maybe he could even make up for lost time today and chalk up a few more hours of work later tonight. Something told him he'd be in for another sleepless night anyway. He needed to keep busy. Work off his restlessness.

If somehow he only could.

Vanessa. He picked up his hammer and sauntered across the deck, thinking. That afternoon, for a moment or two, he'd been afraid she might lose it completely. Why hadn't she listened to him? Though he'd never enlisted in a branch of the military, he was definitely in the know when he'd cautioned her about that copter. The Coast Guard radioman operated a lot like a police dispatcher alerting a patrol car. The circumstances might be different, but the principles were the same.

Thank God, she'd managed to get a hold of herself. He might be a cop, yet he wasn't made of steel. His stomach always did turn to mush whenever he saw a woman go to pieces. But was pity the only reason he'd ended up kissing her? Or had he given in to the lust stirring inside of him?

Their kiss had been dynamite, leaving him wanting for more. He chewed on his lower lip and considered a moment longer. Physical attraction? Well, she certainly wasn't the first woman he'd ever been attracted to. Yep, mere attraction. *That* he could handle.

But love and commitment? Family and responsibilities? Forget it! Love only spelled trouble with a capital T.

*****

"Lands sake, child, how tired you look," Ruby announced after Vanessa had returned to the lodge. "Let me fix you a spot of tea. I've been keepin' supper warm for you too." Ruby ushered her into the half-kitchen behind the lodge office, equipped with a small refrigerator, a hot plate, and a pedestal table with two ladder-back chairs.

"You're awesome," Vanessa said as she helped herself to a bowl of beef stew, then sat down at the table. Fatigue and worry had dulled her appetite, coupled with the fresh emotions tumbling through her head. Lowell's kiss had left her breathless and confused. Why had she melted in his arms that way, allowed him to kiss her? Why had she so foolishly given in to her need for him?

"Did you and Lowell turn up any clues?" the older woman wanted to know.

Vanessa bit her lip. "I'm afraid not." She told her about their boat trip across the channel, how they'd searched the peninsula, and her conversation with the officers at the Coast Guard station. She didn't mention her reignited feelings for Lowell. She wasn't prepared to admit to anyone, not even Ruby, the way he was affecting her. It had been wrong in the first place, she decided with a firm mental kick. And she had no choice but to put a screeching halt to her feelings before they spiraled out of control.

Besides, in the lengthening shadows, beneath the flood-lights on the back deck, he was hard at work again. She couldn't chance he might stop working and overhear. "What a day you've had," Ruby crooned. "You must try to get a good night's sleep, child. Why, I'm surprised I'm not having to scrape you up off the floor right now."

"I do plan to turn in early," Vanessa said. "But I've been waiting to talk to you."

"Yes, we're long overdue."

A man on the TV announced the time, half past eight. The melodic strains of a classical song soon followed.

"Ah, *Meditation from Thais,*" Vanessa said, recognizing it immediately. "You made me perform that for my first big recital."

Ruby smiled reminiscently as she filled the kettle with tap water. "How well I remember. And I kept telling you, play it appassionato, play it from the heart. Some say this is the world's most romantic love song."

"That you did." Vanessa tipped her head back and closed her eyes as the hauntingly beautiful swells rose and fell. Once again, a picture of Lowell floated up in her mind. The realization that she was powerless to erase it frightened her. Quickly she opened her eyes, sprang to her feet, and snapped off the TV.

"Why did you do that?" Ruby asked, her face registering surprise.

"Headache," Vanessa lied.

The tea kettle began to shrill. Ruby removed it promptly and poured the steaming water into Mama's rose-patterned tea pot. "Well now, you just enjoy a nice soothing cup of this herb tea. It'll help relax you."

"Thanks, Ruby." Vanessa met Ruby's look of concern and managed a smile. Her mother would be pleased, knowing someone was still enjoying her china dishes.

Ruby and Mom were so alike. Though they'd both seen hard-times, they appreciated a few delicate touches in their lives, like fine china, classical music, and time out for tea. Only problem was, these fineries didn't seem to match well with the sounds of Lowell's hammering and sawing outside. As Vanessa sipped her tea, the sweet smell of mint wafted about her. "Ruby?"

"Yes, child?" She sat down on the opposite side of the table.

"Did you happen to see Dad at the bait shop the other morning before he disappeared?"

"Yes, I did. Eldon often called it his second home." She shook her head. "He was just like clock-work."

Vanessa stabbed at a carrot. "Was he alone? Just as Clinton seems to think?"

"Now *that* I don't know for sure. I recall having to run back to the kitchen because Pete, the cook, said he needed a hand at the grill." Her voice broke as she lifted her tea cup in midair. "That's the last I saw of your papa, I'm afraid. I can't say what happened after that."

"His old cronies who were hanging out there, did they seem on good terms with Dad? Was everyone getting along?"

"I would imagine so. I doubt if Eldon has an enemy on the face of the earth. He might sound like an ornery old cuss at times, but everyone knows keep down he's nothing but a soft-hearted teddy bear." She smiled faintly. "And a comedian too. We could always count on him to come up with the funniest one-liners."

"So nothing appeared unusual?"

"Not that I could tell." Ruby folded her arms across her chest and added, "But you won't believe what some folks are saying."

Vanessa swallowed a mouthful of stew, then leaned closer. "What? That he took his own life? Just like the Coast Guard officers suggested when they stopped by last night?"

"No. Heavens, no. Anyone who knew Eldon wouldn't think that for a minute. Some folks are saying he may have been visited by aliens and taken away. Now don't that beat all?"

"Yes." Vanessa fought back rising panic. Had the island residents given up on her father already? Had she? No, not for a minute. She might have come close to it that very afternoon on the beach with Lowell, but never again.

Vanessa stared at the clumped tea leaves clinging to the bottom of her cup. "And as for me, I have my own theories. I can't believe Dad lost control of the boat and drowned. Rough seas never bothered him. Why, those waves would have to get awfully wild before he'd even lower his stabilizers."

"My thoughts exactly," Ruby agreed. "Matt's often said Eldon could move about in his boat as sure-footed as a blindfolded alley cat."

For the next several minutes, they sat in companionable silence. The ticking of the clock above the stove mingled with the sounds of Lowell hammering. hen a loud thud.

"Ouch!"

Vanessa winced as Lowell's exclamation gave way to a lengthy silence. At last he started hammering again. She pulled her attention back to Ruby.

"I hope you had an easy time today in the office," Vanessa said. "You can't imagine what a big help it is."

"This place is no different than running Eagle Point," Ruby replied with a wave of her hand. "Vacationers are all alike. The young ones with kids want plenty of action, the single-type are on the prowl for romance, and the old folks ask for nothing more than peace and quiet, and the promise of a good restaurant close by."

"Peace and quiet with that racket outside?" Vanessa asked with dry amusement. Somehow, despite her comment, Ruby appeared oblivious to the commotion. "Sounds as if you should've never retired, Ruby. You know the business better than anyone on the island."

The woman's eyes twinkled. "Of course. But the trick is convincing Clinton of that. I told him that I was good booking appointments for the entire afternoon, but that old geezer insisted he take over. I guess his gang hauled in their limit of clams in no time, so the trip ended sooner than anyone expected. Anyway, we'll just let him sit out there and play boss while you and I visit."

The conversation flowed between them as Ruby asked about Vanessa's position at the university and Vanessa, in turn, inquired further about Ruby's job at the bait shop.

"Sometimes I feel like I'm playing den mother to all those fishermen," Ruby confided. "Every one of them wants a soft shoulder to cry on when times are tough. The Doughnut Hole Club, they call themselves. And guess who keeps those doughnuts coming."

Vanessa nodded, smiling wanly.

Ruby took a sip of tea and went on, "Oh, don't get me wrong. I'm glad I finally stopped managing the cabins and went to work part-time at the bait shop instead. It was just getting too much for me. I couldn't even leave for a quick run into town without finding someone to come fill in while I was gone. At least now, I've turned over all the repairs to the new management. Let them take care of whatever help and supplies they might need and then send me the bill at the end of each month." Ruby stopped to bush a wisp of gray hair from her forehead. "Should've done it long time ago after my hubby died, but I guess I wasn't ready. Being on my own, letting go of Eagle Point was like giving up my last claim to family."

"I get it," Vanessa said. The mention of family tugged at her heart.

Ruby's eyes widened. "Oh! I almost forgot! Matt stopped by to look at Clinton's new spinning reel this afternoon, just like Clint wanted him to. Matt said to tell you he was sorry he missed your call and that you should keep trying. He feels terrible about your papa. I can tell it by that troubled look in his eyes."

"Hey, what's going on in here?" Clinton poked his head through the French doors separating the office from the kitchen. "How come I'm not invited to the tea party?"

"Oh, you old fool," Ruby answered, a quick blush spreading over her face. "Can't a couple of long-lost friends share a little girl talk without you men folk getting your ears all out of kilter?"

He shrugged, his eyes round with mock innocence. "Why of course, my dear. I do beg your pardon. Far be it from me to break up a good old-fashioned gab session." With a tip of his hat, he turned to leave.

"You're not interrupting anything," Vanassa exclaimed, jumping up to offer her chair. By all means, sit down." She caught sight of Ruby and Clinton exchanging tentative glances, the mischievous sparkle in her uncle's eyes. Vanessa felt unexpectedly light-hearted. This sign of budding romance between Ruby and her uncle momentarily blotted out her fatigue.

"Ruby, offer him some stew," she coaxed. "There's some left, isn't there?"

The older woman jumped up and headed to the counter, fluttering about like a hummingbird zeroing in on fragrant blossom. "Of course."

"Oh, don't bother," Clinton put in quickly. "I had my supper hours ago." Despite his refusal, he sat down. Now for my exit, Vanessa thought, delightfully smug. Let the two love birds be alone.

"Excuse me." It was Lowell standing in the doorway. He turned to Clinton and said, "I thought I heard you talking in here. I need to ask a quest—" He bit off his last words as his gaze swept the room. "Uh, am I interrupting anything?"

"Not at all. Come in," Clinton piped up.

Lowell moved towards Vanessa, so near she had to fight back waves of longing. The sight of his rippling biceps reminded her of his strong protective embrace only hours earlier. She caught a whiff of his clean, masculine scent and alarming heat rose up inside her.

"Yes, by all means!" Ruby put in, hurrying to him with outstretched arms. "My, every time I see you, Lowell, I can't get over what a handsome lad you've turned into."

He planted a kiss on her cheek. "And you, Ruby, grow more lovely we each passing day."

Clinton cleared his throat, then smiled. "You must be hungry, Lowell. Help yourself to some of Ruby's chow."

"No thanks, I can't," Lowell replied. "There's too much work to do."

"You young people!" Ruby clucked her tongue again. "Don't you ever know when to quit?"

Vanessa's gaze focused on the blood-stained wad of Kleenex he'd wrapped around his thumb. It was obvious his injury had been minor.

"Need a Band-Aid for your owie?" she couldn't resist teasing. "Nurse Vanessa to the rescue. What'll be? Batman? Donald Duck? Oh yes, I almost forgot. Teenage Ninja Turtles are the rage these days."

"Knock it off," he bantered back, darting her a dimpled smile. "My thumb will be fine. I came to ask Clinton a question, not to play your silly games."

"Okay, shoot," Clinton prompted.

"I'm almost ready to start that new addition to the deck." Lowell held up a frayed sheet of paper. "But somehow these plans and what we talked about earlier don't jibe."

Clinton started to rise, but Vanessa quickly intervened. If she and Lowell didn't get out of here, that little bit of magic she'd sensed between the elderly couple might burst like a soap bubble.

"Hold on," she said, placing a gently restraining hand on Clinton's shoulder. "Sit right back down. I'll take care of Lowell. I was just about ready to leave anyway."

She breezed across the tiny kitchen, meeting Lowell's perplexed gaze. "In the office," she hissed. "We can talk in the office."

"Since when did you become an expert in repairing decks?" he asked once they were safely beyond the couple's earshot.

"I didn't."

"Well then, what's on your mind? You said you intended to take care of me." He grinned. "Or am I simply the object of your latest cause? Nurse Vanessa to the rescue."

She crossed her arms, mildly irked at his attempt to humor her. "Don't be so dense. Have you already forgotten what I told you this morning about Ruby and Clinton?"

"No. But how was I to know what was going on? And more to the point, how was I to know you've appointed yourself official match-maker at Kaloch Bay Lodge?"

"The sparks between Ruby and Clinton have been burning for a long time. I'm just making sure no one stands in their way." She jabbed her finger at his chest. "And that means you too, Maxwell."

"Oh yeah?" He shot her a wicked look.

"Yeah."

"Look," Lowell said, sobering. "I think you ought to let well enough alone. Ruby and Clinton were adults long before either one of us were gleams in our daddies' eyes. Leave the romance bit up to them."

"I just want them to be happy. Both of them . . ." A sudden thought jarred her. If she truly believed that romance could bring happiness to Ruby and her uncle, then why did she believe the opposite in regards to herself? Could some small secret part of her yearn for love and commitment?

The landline phone jangled, slicing through her thoughts. Vanessa gave a start, then moved quickly to answer it, but the ringing stopped. She strained to hear. Her uncle had picked up the phone in the kitchen and was talking to someone in terse phrases. She knew in an instant something was wrong.

Motioning for Lowell to follow, she made her way back just as her uncle was hanging up. Clinton's face was as white as the dishtowel in Ruby's hand.

"What is it?" Vanessa blurted out.

"That was an officer from the Coastguard operations center."

"And?" Lowell prompted from behind, placing a firm hand on Vanessa's shoulder.

"Someone has broken into Eldon's boat." Clinton's voice shook. "His heart pills are missing."

Chapter Five

"Oh, no," Vanessa gasped. The room seemed to spin about her. "Dad's been kidnapped."

"Let's not jump to conclusions," Clinton said shakily. "After all, none of us have gotten a ransom note."

"But if Eldon was the one who took the pills," Ruby pointed out, "which he'd have every right to do since they belong to him in the first place, then why is he staying away like this? Unless, of course, someone is forcing him to."

Clinton, still ghostly pale, rubbed his chin. "Maybe there's been foul play. Maybe someone's taken my brother's pills to make it look as if he's alive, when he really isn't. And even if Eldon did go back for those pills himself, how would he have gotten to Bradshaw Island without his boat?" Clinton turned to Lowell who'd remained stonily silent. *"You're the cop. What do you think?"*

A flicker of indecision passed over Lowell's face. "Those are all valid questions, but right now I just can't answer them." He squared his jaw. "Still, this could be a turning point. I think I'd better head into town first thing tomorrow morning and have a talk with the sheriff."

As the conversation bounced back and forth, fading into Vanessa's thoughts, she wandered to the window at the back of the small kitchen and stared woodenly outside. *Kidnapped.* She felt her entire body trembling as the possibility gripped her. But who? Why? Overcome with despair, she slumped against the window frame.

"Vanessa." Lowell's voice snatched her back.

She turned slowly around. "What?"

"You're not looking too well. Maybe you'd better turn in. It's late. Nearly midnight."

"I'm fine now." She drew in a breath and squared her shoulders. She could tell by the look on his face, he didn't believe her.

"Listen to me," he went on, his eyes riveting on hers. "I don't want you to go searching for Eldon unless I'm with you. Next time you fire up your boat and head out into the Sound, don't do it without me. You're Eldon's only next of kin . . . and if he has indeed been taken hostage, then you could be next. There're too many isolated islands out there, too many places where you could run into trouble."

"Aren't you carrying this a little too far?" she asked as she dismissed his warning. "I mean, of course there could be danger, but if you asked me, you're just dwelling on the dark side. Perhaps more than is necessary."

"That's my job, Vanessa." He leveled her with his gaze.

"And what if you're not available?"

"No what ifs." His voice hardened. "I mean it. You must give me your word."

"But there's so much work here. You've got to help Clinton. You just said so yourself a little while ago." A little voice inside reminded her that only yesterday she'd practically pleaded with him to accompany her. Why now, admittedly even in the face of possible danger, was she trying to talk him out of it? Had their kiss on the beach unlocked too many unsettling feelings? Feelings she wasn't prepared to face?

"Vanessa, don't argue with Lowell," Clinton jumped in. "He knows what he's talking about. And the work here can take a back seat right now."

She heaved a sigh, then swallowed hard. "All right."

"So it's a promise?" Lowell asked.

She shifted beneath his steady gaze. "Yes."

"Good." His eyes softened as they held hers for an immeasurable moment. What was it she was reading in them? Concern? Fear? *Tenderness?*

If she kept looking at him like this, she was bound to go crazy. Jerking away, she strode back to the window and stared hard into the night. A web of emotions rose inside of her with new dread, greater than she'd ever known, matched by the fragile expectancy that Eldon Paris may still be alive.

*****

Vanessa slept fitfully. Her restless dreams about Eldon wove in and out like dark, fluid shadows intermingled with images of Lowell's ruggedly handsome face. Why did he have to be here right now, complicating an already complicated situation? Why couldn't it be *anyone* other than Lowell?

She awoke the next morning at the first light of dawn, utterly drained. More questions plagued her. If someone had taken her father's medication with the intent of keeping him well, why?

Then, too, Clinton had made a good point about there being no ransom note. What if Dad *had* suffered a heart attack and drowned, and the missing pills were a coincidence? At any rate, she still hadn't been successful getting a hold of Matt. Surely he would want to know about the latest developments.

She unlocked the door to the office, sat down at the desk and pulled her cell phone from her back pocket. She punched in the number to the cabins, only to learn Matt was still unavailable.

Several hours later, she spied Lowell bounding up the front steps of the lodge, two at a time. For a split second, she felt a disturbing warmth wash over her, then snapped her attention back.

"Did you find anything out?" she asked as she rushed onto the porch to meet him.

"No, nothing about Eldon. But I did learn the Coast Guard has called off the search."

"It's only been three days! Dad was reported missing late Sunday evening. Why so soon?"

"As far as the Coast Guard is concerned, three days are *not* soon. Normally, under these circumstances, they don't look longer than a couple of days."

"But what about the missing heart pills? Isn't that enough evidence to keep them searching?"

His face was grim. "I'm afraid not."

Fresh despair washed over her. "So everyone's given up, haven't they?"

"Not everyone, Nessie. The Sheriff and wildlife authorities are still looking," he continued, his words measured. "And don't forget the Eagle Scouts and skin-diving clubs and everyone else who's gotten involved. The locals on this island have known Eldon much too long to pull out yet."

"Yes, you're right." She tipped her chin. "I have to keep holding onto that. I can't let go. And speaking of the locals, that reminds me." She told him about her futile attempts to talk to Matt. "I'm going to drive into town and look up some of Dad's other old cronies," she continued. "Someone, somewhere just has to have a clue."

"So that means you're not planning to go looking for Eldon today?"

"No." She hesitated. "I'll wait till tomorrow."

"All right then." He tweaked her chin, his expression closed. "Just be careful."

*****

The rest of that week, Vanessa made repeated trips into town. Though everyone was sympathetic, offering their good wishes, none could offer any help, not even her father's friends at the bait shop.

Her continued efforts to contact Matt were also met with discouraging results. Every time she called the Eagle Point cabins, Dolly told her in a detached voice that Matt was out guiding another fishing excursion. Likewise, each time Matt attempted to return Vanessa's call, she and Lowell were busy scouring the shorelines, beaches, and hidden coves again, continuing their own search.

"Let Vanessa know I'll be at the cabins next Monday morning," Matt had reiterated to Ruby with each repeated attempt. "No fishing trips that day, and plenty of work piling up on the property."

The following Monday morning, she drove her car down the meandering roadway that cut through the rural country-side, marked by cornfields and apple orchards. A light drizzle began to fall. Through her open window she sniffed the fresh smells of rain against asphalt. A brown and white cow, grazing behind a cyclone fence, lifted its head to stare at her.

Yet the idyllic landscape contrasted with her unsettled thoughts. It'd been one week now since she'd come back to the island. A week and one day since anyone had last seen her father. And with each hour that passed, she had no choice but to admit that the likelihood of finding him alive seemed more remote. Still, the thought of Dad's missing medication nagged at the back of her mind. It didn't make sense.

She came upon a slow-moving car ahead—a local, no doubt—and drummed her fingers impatiently against the steering wheel. The island speed limit never exceeded 45 and the driver ahead of her was cruising perhaps half that speed.

At the sight of a familiar row of mailboxes, Vanessa slowed the car, then followed the winding drive that led to the cabins. There were the wild blackberry vines rambling on each side of the lane, the blackberries she and Ruby used to pick together and make into golden-crusted cobblers after they'd finished their music lessons in summer. Vanessa could almost taste their sweet-tart deliciousness.

A circular driveway sloped down to the log cabin office. More memories. White Priscilla curtains adorned the front windows of the office, the window boxes were brimming with scarlet geraniums. Though Vanessa had never considered herself the ruffles and lace type, she'd always admired those curtains. Perhaps it was because Ruby had sewn them herself, making certain they were always freshly laundered and crisply starched.

Coming to a stop in the narrow parking strip beneath a grove of evergreens, Vanessa cut the motor, then glanced towards the pier. About a dozen cabin cruisers, several fishing boats, two Boston Whalers, and a yacht were tied to the dock. In the distance, wafting across the water, she heard music.

The office inside appeared empty. Vanessa spied a small bell on the counter and rang it. Finally a woman appeared—a tall, striking woman in her late twenties, Vanessa guessed, with a mane of thick blond hair and a figure that would make any beauty pageant contestant envious. Could this be Dolly? Josh Buckler's cousin? Though Clinton's mention of her had been nondescript, something told Vanessa the answer was yes. Dolly was a looker. Good thing Lowell didn't come here with me, she thought, then quickly wondered why that should even matter to her.

"Welcome to Eagle Point Tourist Cabins," the woman purred. "May I help you?"

"Yes. You must be Dolly."

"That's right. And who are you?"

"I'm Vanessa Paris. Eldon Paris's daughter. I've talked to you on the phone when I tried to get in touch with Matt."

The woman's eyes widened momentarily, then she assumed her original honey-smooth poise. "And he told you to come here today?"

"Yes. Where can I find him, please?" Vanessa pulse raced with anticipation. What if something had unexpectedly taken Matt away again? What if his plans had changed?

"He's working out back," Dolly said coolly, waving her hand in the direction of the dock. "But don't take up too much of his time. Josh don't take kindly to anyone interrupting him."

Dismissing the implication behind Dolly's remark, Vanessa thanked her, hurried outside and followed the graveled walkway to the dock. The sun had pierced the layer of clouds and the showers had stopped, but large glistening drops of rain still clung to the low growing vegetation alongside the trail.

Suddenly a movement off to the side caught her eye, the flash of pruning shears catching a beam of light. There was Matt trimming a long arborvitae hedge.

"Matt!" she hollered, walking quickly towards him.

He set down his shears and met her with opened arms. His salt-and-pepper hair had turned white and worry-lines etched his face.

"Well, well! If it isn't my old buddy's little girl. You must've got my message. I'm sorry you had to call so many times." He enveloped her in a massive hug. "Did you come here alone?" he asked, pulling back and glancing over his shoulder. "Lowell isn't with you?"

"No, he's back at the lodge helping Uncle Clint."

"I hear he went into police work after leaving the island."

"Well, actually a few years after that. First he finished college."

"Oh."

"So how have you been?" she asked, sending Matt a quick smile. "It seems like forever since I last saw you and Fern."

"Too busy for my own good." He swallowed hard. "Is . . . is there any word yet about Eldon?" His eyes met hers and a sudden grief seemed to spring from their depths as he added, "You must be sick with worry."

"Yes." Her chin trembled. "We're all so worried. Last Tuesday Uncle Clint got a phone call from the Coast Guard Operations Center." She told him about the missing heart medication. "That's one of the reasons I was trying to get in touch with you. To tell you that. And to also ask you some questions."

"What is it you need to know?"

"Did you see much of Dad before he disappeared? Was he depressed? Anxious? In some kind of trouble?" Again she presented the questions that had been tumbling inside her head.

Matt's eyes darted nervously towards the dock. "I've been spending so much time here, trying to help Josh and Dolly get on their feet, I'm afraid Eldon and I haven't gotten together to do much fishing these days. I really can't tell you what's been going on with your pop."

"I don't understand any of this," Vanessa said. "None of it makes a bit of sense."

"So true." Matt sighed and shook his head. "Stuff like this isn't supposed to happen on our peaceful little island." He motioned to the boathouse. I have to string up some line on a few fishing poles. Josh likes to have them ready for the guests who forget to bring their own from home. We can talk more while I work."

Vanessa choked back her disappointment as she fell into step alongside him. Obviously, though Matt meant well, he wasn't going to be much help either.

As they came nearer to the dock, the music grew louder, a blaring, syncopated beat punctuated by loud talking. Vanessa spied two bare-chested men sitting on the top deck of the yacht she'd noticed earlier. From inside came peals of laughter.

"What's going on over there?" she asked Matt as they paused to take in the scene.

"That's one of our more well-to-do clients," he answered matter-of-factly. "Josh is down in the cabin. The yacht owner threw a big bash last night and they apparently don't have enough sense to know when to call it quits."

She darted Matt a sympathetic look. "No wonder you must work so hard around here. My guess would be you're the *only* one working. And by the way, how is Fern? Has there been any improvement since her stroke?"

"She barely recognizes anyone, even me. The paralysis has affected one entire side, and despite all the therapy, there doesn't appear to be much improvement."

Vanessa shook her head sadly as a picture of Matt's vivacious, fun-loving wife came to her. Fern had cooked many a hearty pot roast dinner for Vanessa's family in years past. "How terrible that must be for you," Vanessa said.

"Yep. Life does take some unexpected turns, now don't it?" Matt spoke in a distant voice. "And the nursing home costs are enough to blow any hard-working man right out of the saddle."

He fell silent as they started walking again, then entered the boat house. The pungent odors of raw fish mingled with the smells of creosote.

"Redding!" A brusque male voice boomed seemingly out of nowhere. "Git back to work! What do you think this is? Time out for tea?"

Vanessa looked up to see a beefy man glowering down at them. Next to him stood another man, pot-bellied and balding, swigging down a can of beer.

"And who's the little lady?" the first man asked, a slow grin spreading across his red-bearded face.

"Vanessa Paris. Eldon Paris's daughter," Matt replied evenly. "Vanessa, meet Josh Buckler. And his business partner, Amos Matthews."

Vanessa gave them a cursory nod, refraining from extending her hand.

"Well, well, I do declare," Josh bellowed. "She even looks like her old man. Don't you say, Amos?" Josh reached down with massive hands and began massaging one side of her neck while Amos rocked back on his heels and nodded in agreement.

She pushed Josh away, then took two steps backwards.

"Now hold your horses, Buckler," Matt cut in as he sidled protectively next to Vanessa. "Don't get no ideas about this young lady. I've known her almost as long as I've known her father. Besides, she's got a cop staying close by the lodge. You mess with her and you're asking for trouble."

"Bug off, old man."

"*You* bug off, Buckler. Keep your hands off my buddy's little girl, you hear? You've got your women back on the boat."

"I do beg your pardon," Josh said mockingly. "I must've lost my head for a minute. After all, we believe in treating celebrities around here with lots of *ree-spect*, now don't we, Amos?"

"You bet," the second man answered with a sardonic grin. "Celebrities who visit the Eagle Point cabins get nothing but the best."

"Celebrities?" Vanessa shot back, her gaze flitting from Josh to Amos. "What are you talking about?"

"You! Who else?" Josh roared with laughter. "The famous daughter of the long-lost fisherman, the old granddaddy himself of Tawanya Island."

"I need some time alone with Matt," Vanessa said pointedly, ignoring his insults. And goodness only knows, he probably needs a break. Judging from what I see going on here, he doesn't get much help from either of you!"

Josh spat on the ground, then spread his hands wide. "Hey, simmer down, miss. You need to talk to old Redding here, then go ahead. Who said anyone was stopping you?"

"Fine. Now please leave us alone." She gritted her teeth and faced Matt squarely, trying to block out the feeling of Josh's gaze still boring through her.

*****

Totally frustrated, Vanessa drove away from the Eagle Point cabins. Talking with Matt, she hadn't learned a clue. And the only impressions she'd formed about Josh Buckler and Amos was that she disliked them intensely. Deciding to stop by the bait shop for a hot cup of coffee, she followed the main road into town. The road wound gently down a wooded hillside, thick with oak and madrone. In no time the marina came into view. A grid work of docks and assorted boats stretched out from the rocky beach. The combined bait shop and small café, a low sprawling building with gray weathered shakes, stood in the foreground.

Inside the cafe, Vanessa glanced about. A handful of bearded men wearing fishing garb and black rubber boots were vacating the booth near the front entrance.

She felt as if she were moving though a repetitious bad dream, stuck in slow motion. Yet during her several trips here this past week, she'd never seen these men before. Maybe they could help her.

"Excuse me," she said, striding towards them. She quickly introduced herself and asked whether they knew her father.

They only shook their heads, their faces vague. "We're just vacationers," a guy dressed in a red-and-black wool jacket apologized. "But we heard about your father. Everyone's heard. Good luck, miss. Sure wish we could help."

A lump rose in Vanessa's throat as she nodded wordlessly, forcing a polite smile. Their response was becoming far too familiar.

After the men left, she sat down at a small table, covered with a yellow vinyl cloth. She focused her gaze out the window and watched a black wharf cat bolting down scraps of food a fisherman had tossed its way.

Unexpectedly her thoughts turned again to Lowell. Before she'd left that morning, they'd exchanged only a few brief words. He said he'd be busy doing odd jobs around the lodge until she returned, then they would go looking for Eldon again.

"This time, let's take one of the kayaks," he'd suggested. "That way we can get into some of the smaller coves and more shallow waters."

She'd readily agreed.

Staring hard into the freestanding wood stove, she watched the crackling flames dance across the top of three charred logs. The warmth, coupled by the mouth-watering smells of freshly made doughnuts, enveloped her in a false welcoming cocoon. Yes, the Doughnut Hole Club, Ruby had called the folks who frequented here.

Such a homey, ordinary scene. Was it a similar ordinary scene the morning Dad had stopped by here before disappearing forever?

"Coffee?" A waitress's voice cut through her thoughts.

"Yes, please." Vanessa looked up and saw a young woman, barely twenty, perhaps, looking down at her.

"I'm sorry about your daddy," the waitress went on as she plunked down an empty mug and filled it with the rich dark brew. She was dressed in a red two-piece dress topped by a robin's egg blue apron.

"I couldn't help overhearing your conversation with those men," the waitress prattled on. "I don't usually eavesdrop, you know. But as they said, too, everyone around has heard about your daddy."

"Thanks for your concern," Vanessa replied shakily. She lifted the mug to her lips and took a sip.

"My name's Sally," the waitress went on. "I started work about a month ago, though I stayed home most of last week with the flu." She paused to tuck an unruly black curl behind one ear. "But I *was* here the day your daddy left."

"You were?" Vanessa's heart leaped with anticipation.

"Yes. I thought it seemed a little strange that morning when your daddy came in with someone different."

"What do you mean by *someone different*?"

"Well, you see, your daddy always used to grab a bite to eat here with this tall, good-looking guy. A guy with a mop of dark blond hair and the dreamiest blue eyes."

"Did he usually wear a black leather jacket?"

"Yeah, I think so. And he had really cool build. A cop, I think, or at least he used to be." She rolled her eyes. "Wow! Would I ever like to get pulled over by a cop who looked like him."

Vanessa pushed back a twinge of annoyance. Undoubtedly Lowell commanded that kind of attention from women no matter where he went. "But of course, the cop wasn't with my father that morning, right?"

"Oh, no. I was just getting to that. There was another man, someone I'd never seen before. He and your daddy were arguing."

"About what?"

"I only caught snatches. Something about the overseas black market, but that's about all I could hear."

Vanessa gulped. The overseas black market? How could have her father gotten mixed up in anything like that?

"What did the man look like?" she asked.

Sally shrugged, snapping her chewing gum. "I can't remember any of the details except that he was sort of big."

"Was he young? Old?"

"I can't remember that part either. I've only been working here a couple of weeks, see, and my mind was on lots of things. Like keeping my prices straight. And trying to get the food out piping hot."

Vanessa's stomach twisted into a hard knot. "Please, Sally. Think hard. Try to remember even the slightest detail about the man. Anything would help. Anything at all."

"That's it, I'm afraid."

"Are you sure there was just one person?"

"Yes, that much I know. All I remember thinking at the time was I wished your daddy had come in with the other guy instead. What a hunk. Come to think of it, I haven't seen him around here since."

Vanessa gulped down her coffee and bounded to her feet. "Excuse me, but I've got to run! I've got to talk to Lowell!"

"Who's Lowell?" The waitress inclined her head to one side, her mouth slightly parted.

"The cop!" Vanessa thrust a five-dollar bill into Sally's hand, made a hasty exit, and dashed to her car.

Chapter Six

"Where's Lowell?" Vanessa asked Ruby breathlessly back at the lodge. Ruby was sitting in one of the two dark green wicker rocking chairs on the front porch, trying to contain a wiggling Toby in her arms.

"He went into town for another load of lumber," she answered. "He also said he might swing back to the sheriff's department again, then go to the Coast Guard station. What's the matter?"

Sitting down in the other chair, Vanessa told her about what the young waitress had said, purposefully leaving out her glowing description of Lowell's physical assets. "I need to talk to him, Ruby. See if her story makes any sense to Lowell."

Ruby chuckled. "Ah, don't pay too much attention to Sally. That girl's got an imagination that won't quit. Why, I hear before she got into waitressing, she tried a stint in Hollywood." She paused, fiddling with a button on her blouse as she stared off into the distance. "But I am a bit worried about something else."

"Oh?"

"I think there's something going on at the cabins. I'm picking up strange vibes. Perhaps I should be talking to Lowell also."

"What do you mean . . . strange vibes?" Alarm filled Vanessa's voice.

"Last night, after I'd gone back to the property to pick blackberries, I overheard Josh and Dolly bickering by the boathouse. It was only minutes before they met up with all those slick-looking folks you just mentioned, the ones partying on the yacht."

"And then what happened?" Given her encounter with the anything-but-slick-looking Josh Buckler, Vanessa couldn't imagine his friends being high class.

"I could only hear snatches, but it was enough to worry me," Ruby went on, lowering her voice. "Josh sounded real threatening and Dolly talked like she was scared out of her wits. Money problems, I think. But then their voices faded, and I couldn't make out the rest. I'm not sure what could be wrong. Every month the rent comes in right on time, and Josh is turning over his part of the consignment we agreed on, so I suppose whatever's going on is none of my business—"

The phone rang inside the office, cutting off Ruby's next words. "I'll get it." She set the dog down and got to her feet.

Vanessa settled back in her chair. The tightly woven wicker creaked beneath her as mulled over what Ruby had just said. Josh and Dolly certainly weren't the first to argue about money. Her experience in counseling had taught her that.

The sound of Ruby's voice sliced through Vanessa's thoughts. "For you, dear!"

"Okay! I'll be right there!"

Cupping her hand over the receiver before handing it to Vanessa, Ruby murmured, "She says it's long distance. And she sounds very young."

"Oh, Ms. Paris!" Carmen wailed into the phone a moment later. "It seems like forever since you've been away from the counseling center. All us kids . . . we're really bummed out about that." Vanessa had considered giving them her cell phone number, but then decided not to. The lodge phone was good enough.

"I know, Carmen. I know." She paused, biting her lip. "How are you?"

"Okay. Except for the usual stuff about me and Robert. But anyway . . . I was just calling to see when you're coming back. Next week, maybe?"

Vanessa heaved a sigh. "I don't think so, Carmen. There's been a couple of recent developments about my father, but nothing conclusive yet. I'm afraid I must stay here a while longer."

"Oh. That's cool. About the developments, I mean. But not cool about your staying. lease come home just as soon as you can, okay? Like we miss you. And need you. I mean, *really* need you. Mr. Collins, that guy who's leading the discussion groups while you're gone, he's okay and all. But the kids here asked me to call you. We don't feel good about confiding in him like we do with you."

Sighing again, Vanessa felt as if she were in the middle of a tug of war. She simply had to be here for Dad's sake, but the kids needed her too. "I'll do my best, Carmen. Just give Mr. Collins a fair chance, okay?"

"Sure! But hurry back anyway. See ya!"

"Bye."

"That was one of the girls from my support group back in Seattle," Vanessa explained as she and Ruby sat down again on the front porch. "The poor kid's got a heap of problems. Last year her parents divorced. Her younger brother's spent the past two years in a juvenile detention facility, and her on-again, off-again relationship with a boy's who's doing drugs has given her nothing but grief."

"Times have sure changed," Ruby said, shaking her head and clicking her tongue. "Not that there weren't problems back in my day, too, mind you. I guess folks just kept a lot of their dirty underwear locked up in the closet."

"Yes. And sometimes with unfortunate consequences later down the pike," Vanessa answered. She picked up Toby and cuddled him to her chest, thinking back to what Lowell had said about his father. "He might as well have been dead for all the times we never heard from him." Undoubtedly Lowell had formed his own ideas about dysfunctional families.

Toby covered her face with warm, wet licks, temporarily distracting her. "What a darling you are," she murmured. She ran her hand through the dog's silky fur, then scratched him behind one ear. She couldn't help recalling the look of adoration on Lowell's face that night on the sailboat when he'd looked at the dog. Obviously Lowell wasn't so tough and unfeeling after all. Could this furry little bundle be filling a void in Lowell's life? A need for love and companionship?

"Toby is one *spoiled* darling," Ruby said. "Why, already this morning, he's managed to dig up most of Clinton's dahlias in the front flower beds. And when I tried to feed him the can of dog food Lowell left here, he just turned his nose up at it. Seems he'd rather wolf down more of the left-over steak I fed him earlier this morning."

Vanessa laughed, momentarily forgetting Carmen's phone call and her frustration over finding Lowell gone.

"Well, one thing's for sure, this rascal's been cooped up far too long," Ruby hurried on. "When I suggested to Clinton we take him for a walk after you got back, he high-tailed it out of here before you could blink an eye. You'd think I'd suggested a walk down the aisle instead."

"I'm sure my uncle's reluctance to indulge Toby had more to do with his dahlias then with you, Ruby. But don't worry, he'll get over it." She glanced anxiously at the parking lot. "I wonder what's taking Lowell so long? You say he was stopping at the sheriff's too?"

"That's right." Ruby straightened the hem of her pink cardigan sweater and added, "Relax, child. What difference is another half an hour or so gonna make?"

"I suppose not much," Vanessa relented as a now subdued Toby curled up in her lap.

"The way I see it," Ruby continued, "we're mighty lucky to have Lowell here this summer. It's just too bad he can't be more at peace with himself."

Vanessa felt a stab of guilt. "I'm afraid it was *my* idea he get involved looking for Dad. Some vacation for Lowell, right?"

"He would've gotten involved whether you'd asked him or not," the older woman said sagely. "I think he loves your papa almost as much as you do. Considering Lowell's guilt over not going out with him that day, why, I'm afraid it's too much like the other time—" She broke off suddenly.

"What other time?" Vanessa asked. Undoubtedly Lowell had taken Ruby into his confidence and told her the entire story. Perhaps that very morning after Vanessa had left.

The color drained from Ruby's face. "I promised not to say. He said he's not ready to talk about it with anyone else yet. I shouldn't have let that slip."

Vanessa drew in a steadying breath, then released it slowly. "All right then. I'll pretend you didn't." *But if he can talk about it with you, why can't he talk about it with me?* she silently questioned. *I want to help him too. And I've got the skills to do it, if only he'd let me.*

Yet her questions were soon eclipsed by a new realization. Could there be more than mere professional reasons fueling her desire to help Lowell?

One thing she knew for certain. She couldn't stand sitting around waiting for him another minute. Maybe Toby wasn't the only one who needed a brisk walk. Maybe she did too.

"Where's Toby's leash?" Vanessa asked, looking around. Let me walk him so you don't have to worry about it. Maybe we'll take the trail in the woods above the beach, the one that comes out at the public dock. If Lowell comes back while I'm gone, tell him to stick close by."

"I forgot and left the leash in Lowell's sailboat. But wait—I've got the key right here." Ruby fished inside her breast pocket and handed it to Vanessa. "He said he keeps the leash on the shelf next to the daybed. I'll hold onto Toby till you get back."

"Thanks, Ruby. I won't be long."

Minutes later, inside the "Sea Breeze," her gaze strayed about the cabin, taking in Lowell's burgundy lamb's wool sweater on one end of the daybed to a small brass-framed photograph on the shelf next to Toby's leash. She moved closer to get a better look. Three little boys with curly blond hair and cherubic faces were posed like stair steps. The oldest was about eight, the youngest still a toddler, she guessed. Nephews, perhaps? Lowell had never talked about his brothers' children.

She picked up the leash, then forced herself to cross back to the doorway. The faint spicy odor of after-shave hung in the air evoking powerful memories of him. Ever since that day on the beach when he'd kissed her, she couldn't forget the feeling of his lips, his powerful masculine arms pressing her against him.

But it meant nothing, she reminded herself. Nothing more than an attempt to reassure her, though an attempt that could have led to treacherous consequences. Neither of them, she was certain, had bargained for that.

Locking the door, she hurried back to the lodge, retrieved Toby, and headed out. Soon they were striding through the long stretch of forest above the beach. The early afternoon sun was slowly inching its way westward, filtering slanting rays through the treetops. Toby ran eagerly ahead on a long leash, ears flopping as he stopped to sniff at a clump of bracken ferns or to lunge at a grey digger squirrel.

At length, she sat down on a log to rest while Toby lapped at a puddle of rainwater that had filled a rut in the trail. She inhaled deeply the earthy smells of damp humus and lush vegetation. Mottled sunlight filtered in through the trees and tiny yellow wildflowers poked out everywhere.

Yes, she could understand why Lowell had come back to the island to heal himself—even if she didn't fully understand the reason why. She, too, had spent far too long in the crowded city, breathing the fumes of the ever-increasing traffic, setting her alarm clock a little earlier each morning to brave the traffic snarls on the interstate freeway.

Even though she must go back, her work at the university gave her life purpose. Still, she would never sever her ties here. Her family had left her a priceless legacy, this treasure chest of pristine, unspoiled beauty coupled with the precious memories of her childhood and family. But what if now she was truly alone? What if her father was dead too? Unbidden, a tear slipped down her cheek.

"Nessie?" The sound cut through her thoughts, giving her a start.

She looked up and saw Lowell staring down at her. Her heart lurched. "You're back! Finally!"

"Ruby said you and Toby went this way," he said. He sat down beside her—dangerously close—and patted the top of the dog's head. "Hi, there Toby, old boy. You and Vanessa getting to know each other, eh?"

With soft liquid eyes, tail thumping, the dog looked up at Lowell and gave a yip.

Vanessa and Lowell laughed in unison, yet his laughter failed to touch his eyes. He turned back and gave her a long, hard look. "Ruby also said you wanted to talk to me."

"Did she tell you why?"

"Uh-huh." He paused. "And Ruby also had some concerns of her own.

"Yes, I know." She lifted one shoulder. "So what do you think?"

He shook his head and stared down at the ground. "It's hard to say. A lot of folks fight about money. Buckler and Dolly aren't alone when it comes to that. Money problems account for a good share of the call-outs I get involving domestic disputes—that and the notorious love triangle situations. It most likely means nothing..."

"I suppose not. But it does worry Ruby."

"Yes, I realize that. And I don't like to see her worry either. I tried to point out to her that there's no evidence Buckler and his cohorts are doing anything illegal. And as you well know, in a court of law, a man's innocent until proved otherwise."

"Right." She picked up a twig and snapped it into three even pieces. "But I also know I don't care one bit for Josh Buckler." She told him about the way he'd treated her and Matt's attempts to ward him off. "In my opinion, Josh is nothing but low life. A real scum ball, to say the least."

His nostrils flared with indignation. "Good thing *I* wasn't there at the time! I would've told Buckler in no certain terms exactly where to go. And maybe much worse. He had no business laying his hands on you, Vanessa. No business at all!"

"Don't worry. I wasn't about to let myself get in a tight spot. And right now, Josh is the least of my problems." Waving one hand in the air as she talked, she went on to tell him about her brief stopover at the bait shop, and what the waitress had said about her father. "Who do you think could've been at Northshore that morning with Dad?" she asked.

A frown marred his handsome features. "Eldon never mentioned he planned to meet anyone there. As far as I knew, it was supposed to have been just him and me. But don't forget, most of the fishermen on this island have known each other for years."

"True enough. And Dad certainly *did* have a parcel of friends. But if he and this man were arguing, as Sally seemed to think, they certainly weren't on friendly terms right then." A chill tremored through her. "And why were they discussing the overseas black market?"

Lowell laced his fingers together, working them in and out before he spoke. "I don't know. If there's any truth to it, I intend to find out, and I may have my chance this coming Saturday."

"Oh?"

"That's right. When I spoke with the sheriff a little while ago, he gave me a name of an agent from the Fish and Wildlife services on the mainland that might be of some help. I phoned the agent immediately and made an appointment to meet with him this weekend. His headquarters are on the east side of Seattle."

"Can I come too?" she asked.

He eyed her thoughtfully. "You can come with me for the ride, if you like, but when it's time to meet with the agent, that's something I should do alone."

Pushing back a stab of disappointment, she asked. "But why this Saturday? Why can't you meet with him today? Dad's life is at stake! Don't the law enforcement officials realize that?"

Lowell turned to face her, his dark blue eyes beseeching. "Nessie. It's been well over a week since your father disappeared."

"So you're ready to write him off? Just like that?"

"I didn't say that. I'm simply trying to point out that Eldon's chances of being found alive are getting slimmer with each passing day, even if he has been taken ransom."

"No," she said tightly, battling against her own ambivalence. "I just don't buy that. And if you really believe it yourself, then tell me something. Why did you bother to arrange a meeting with the wildlife agent in the first place? Why bother with any of this?"

His jaw twitched. "We have no choice but to consider foul play. And if it's true someone killed Eldon, I want to know who. Justice must be served. That's my job, Vanessa. That's what I've been trained to do."

Foul play. Justice. Anger boiled up inside of her. No matter that Clinton had already considered that, and Lowell had agreed it was a possibility. Right now it seemed as if only Lowell was capable of such cold, calculating thoughts.

"Is that the only reason you want to know what happened to my father?" she shot back. "To satisfy your inquiring mind? To congratulate yourself for another job well done?"

Hurt mingled with despair flashed in his eyes. He jerked his gaze away. A stony silence fell between them.

"I'm sorry," she breathed. Her face burned with shame. I didn't mean that." She balled her hands into fists, overwhelmingly confused. What *did* she want from him? Something more than what he could offer her as an officer of the law?

He turned back to her and met her gaze. "Apology accepted." He chewed on his lower lip, then added. "I wish I had more answers, Vanessa. Help take away some of your pain. But the bottom line is, we can't afford to sit around just wishing."

*****

The remainder of the week, Vanessa tried to ward off the chill that seized her every time she reflected on that conversation with Lowell.

Though she couldn't fully accept his prediction about her father's demise, she also couldn't ignore the truth underscoring it. No one had proved, so far, that Eldon's disappearance *hadn't* involved foul play. And while she and Lowell had continued their search, scouring every shoreline, inlet, and cove, they also had found nothing.

Friday morning Vanessa awoke, her nerves brittle with anticipation. In only twenty-four hours, Lowell would be on his way to the mainland to talk to the wildlife agent. Perhaps this would be the break-through they'd been waiting for.

She showered, dressed quickly, and forced herself to eat a small breakfast in the family headquarters, then stole a few moments to wander alone down to the dock. Rays of sunshine bathed her in dewy warmth as she strolled onto the pier. The Sound appeared as placid and smooth as a mirror. Small sea birds skittered about pecking at the sand. Yet how could the world seem so at peace when her father still hadn't been found?

Farther out, about a dozen vacationers were seated on the deck of the charter boat, their voices rising and falling with eager expectation as Clinton prepared to cast off. A young mother with a toddler in tow hurried down the dock waving and calling out, apparently eager to relay a last-minute message to a couple of men on board.

Normal people. Doing normal, everyday things. Vanessa gave a quick shake of her head, yearning for a return to her own normal life. Yet, she realized once again with sharpening clarity, life for her might never be the same again. No, never.

"We'll be back here by sundown," Clinton hollered to Vanessa. "And oh, there's something I forgot to tell Ruby. The group checking in this afternoon from Bellingham, a family of four by the name of Zussman, called yesterday to tell us they might be late. Don't let her give their unit away."

Vanessa nodded and called back to him. "I'll let her know."

Clinton would be doubling the number of excursions this weekend, Vanessa knew. The Fourth of July crowds had flocked to the island this year in greater numbers than ever.

Clinton fired up the boat and its sudden rumble sliced through her thoughts. She watched it pull away from the dock, chug into the bay, and disappear beyond a tiny island.

Suddenly she spotted Lowell emerge from the sailboat and thread his way down the dock, his stride energetic, purposeful. He was wearing a striped blue-and-white polo shirt and casual white slacks, colors that contrasted the healthy glow of his sun-tanned face. As she drew closer, a new rush of desire swept through her. Inhaling deeply and silently counting to ten, she struggled to regain control. Her anxious feelings were only skyrocketing. But what was it she really feared? Lowell himself or the way he affected her?

Try as she might, she could no longer deny the truth. She was teetering on a perilous edge, allowing her heart to rule her head.

*****

Lowell grinned, lifting a hand in acknowledgment. "My, you're out bright and early this morning."

"I was watching Clinton leave."

His smile quickly faded as his penetrating gaze moved over her. She appeared exhausted, completely done in. There were dark circles under her eyes, a pallor to her skin. Yet somehow that still didn't detract from her beauty, he decided. No, Vanessa was definitely beautiful—and it made him want to take care of her all the more. He'd have to do something to get her mind off Eldon. He'd have to think of something fast.

"You don't look as if you slept well," he said, briefly touching her elbow.

"There's too much on my mind." She smiled, a little too hesitantly, he thought. "But I'm okay. Just fine. I can get along without much sleep."

He paused, tracing one finger down her cheek. "I can't let you get worn to a frazzle over all this."

"Don't worry about me. "

His gaze never faltered from hers. "Why not? I'm practically family, you know."

She tipped up her chin, moving one step back. His nearness was too commanding, and. his sharp, probing gaze, much too unnerving. "So that means you're still thinking about Andy and Dad? That you owe it to them to take care of me?"

"Maybe."

"I said it before, Lowell, and I'll say it again. I'm a big girl now. I can take care of myself."

He ignored her protests as a plan flashed in his mind. Back in high school, he and Andy had given in and finally let the little pest come with them to the old Boy Scout camp on Iffleman island. And when all was said and done, he knew that day had been special to her, though he still couldn't be sure why. Heck, maybe it was because when they'd been kidding around, he'd gone a little crazy and kissed her. Whatever, it really hadn't been any big deal to him, though beforehand, he *had* wondered what she'd do if he should try it.

"Remember that time, Nessie, when you, Andy and I took one of the lodge motor boats to Iffleman Island? It was the end of the summer—a few months after Andy and I'd graduated, I believe—and the last campers had left. No one was around, and we had the whole place to ourselves."

"Yes," she replied, quirking a brow.

"And remember, too, how we fished at that pond in the middle of the island, swung from the old rope swing, then spent the rest of the afternoon on the beach building a gigantic sandcastle. We always said the three of us made a terrific team."

"That we did."

"Too bad we never got around to entering the annual sandcastle contest on the mainland. I'm sure we would've come away with at least one prize."

*****

With alarming alacrity, the picture took shape in Vanessa's mind, a picture of that magical, golden summer's day when the world had been bright and filled with promise.

For once, Andy had given in to her begging that she go along too. And that evening, while a flaming sun sank below the jagged horizon, Lowell had scooped her up in his arms, sprinted down the beach while she'd kicked and hollered, pretending she wanted to be let down.

When he'd finally released her onto the warm, moist sand, he'd stared straight into her eyes and grinned at her with boyish devilment. Then they'd shared a tentative kiss, and at that very moment, she knew she'd fallen in love with him. But then Andy had called to them, and the spell had been broken.

She yearned to admit to Lowell that for as long as she lived, nothing short of a coma could cause her to forget that day. But she didn't dare. She mustn't allow him to suspect how many times these past years she'd reached back for the memory and turned it over in her mind like a delicate, priceless heirloom.

She hesitated, meeting his gaze. So what has this to do with anything?"

"Let's take the afternoon off and sail back there," he answered, eagerness tingeing his voice. "For old time's sake, Nessie."

"Old time's sake?" she parroted, darting him a look. Could Lowell be remembering too? If so, it had to be in a totally male sort of way. To Lowell, the memories undoubtedly centered on how well the fish had been biting that day, and the dare-devil thrill of swooping through the air from a rope that had nearly frayed in two.

"It's obvious you need a little R&R," he insisted, "and I've been itching to see how Sea Breeze handles in a good stiff wind. Besides, Clinton says, now that the deck's done, I owe myself a little time for sailing." He took her hand in his, gently stroking her palm with his thumb.

She wrestled with her rollercoaster feelings. Granted, they'd probably spent nearly a dozen afternoons alone looking for Eldon, but none of their trips had taken them to Iffleman Island.

Returning there would only conjure up too many old feelings, forcing her to face the reality that if she were to fall in love with him again, this time it would involve much more than an adolescent infatuation.

"I'm sorry. I can't go," she answered at last.

"What do you mean you can't go?"

She chewed on her lower lip, floundering for a plausible excuse. "The only time I can justify leaving the lodge is when I'm looking for Dad. It's not right for me to be off sailing somewhere, having a good time. Not now."

"You're wrong. Eldon would agree with me too. He wouldn't hear of that kind of talk. Besides, we'll only be gone a few hours. All I'm asking you is to share one pleasant afternoon with me, Vanessa. Nothing more, I swear."

She opened her mouth to refuse again, but this time the words caught in her throat. His hair reflected glimmers of morning sunlight, making him appear so vital and alive. He inclined his head and allowed a lazy smile to flicker at the corners of his too gorgeous mouth.

"So?" He waited for her reply.

Smiling back, she nodded. "All right. Just for the afternoon." Somehow her resistance had vanished like a snowflake in hot water.

Chapter Seven

The wind tangled Vanessa's hair and snapped her navy-blue jacket as the Sea Breeze puttered out from Kaloch Bay.

Once they were into the Strait of Georgia, well beyond the peninsula and North Jetty where they'd searched for Eldon, Lowell, who was standing at the helm, switched off the motor. "Now that we're in the wide-open spaces, sailing should be perfect," he announced

She slanted him a sidelong glance. The sight of his well-chiseled profile, the gentle curve of his mouth made her pulse race. Maybe it wasn't right setting him up the way she had, but he'd agreed more readily than she'd expected and it'd been worth the trade-off. And as for now, she might as well enjoy herself.

"I thought we'd never get past all those boats filling up the bay," she told him. Behind them, their widening wake cut through the Sound while the gray-green waters turned to a darker blue. "How fast are we moving?"

"Six knots. Slightly under seven miles per hour."

She smoothed back a strand of hair that had whipped across her face. The sailboat rolled and pitched against wind and surf. The mainsail billowed with each new gust.

"Where's Toby?" she asked, glancing back at the cabin.

"He's with Ruby. I hit her up for another day of doggy-sitting."

Vanessa burst into laughter.

"Ruby was more than willing," he was quick to add. "In case you haven't already figured it out, she fell in love with Toby the minute she first saw him. She's still working on Clinton to go with her when she takes Toby for his walks."

"I wish her luck. Clinton's not much into walking these days. Says he gets more than enough exercise working at the lodge."

"Well, I did *my* part." He spread his hands wide. "You can no longer accuse me of standing in their way. I gave her another perfectly legitimate excuse to rope Clinton into a romantic walk on the beach." Sunlight glinted off the bow. Above them, another bald eagle soared, then swooped down into the snag of a tree. Without warning, a Boston Whaler roared from behind, cutting through their conversation. Vanessa looked back and spotted it racing directly towards them. "Look out!" she cried.

Instinctively Lowell thrust out his arm to shield her. The motor boat swerved sharply to the right, its wake showering them with icy spray as it disappeared behind a narrow projection of land.

His face blanched. "Fools!" he muttered through clenched teeth. "Don't they know that a ship under sail always has the right-of-way?"

"That was a close one," she agreed, wiping the spray from her cheeks and forehead with the back of her hand. She reigned in her racing thoughts. For a second she was sure she'd caught a glimpse of Lawrence at the driver's seat. Clinton had given him the entire holiday weekend off. Hadn't she overheard Lawrence telling her uncle he was a novice at boating? Or had his near miss with Lowell's sailboat been somehow intentional?

A chill coursed through her as the familiar warning again echoed. Lowell's a cop. He lives with constant danger. What if someone was out, not to harm Clinton nor herself, but *Lowell*?

Swallowing the fear building in her throat, she forced aside the thought and concentrated on the scenery before her. They were drifting effortlessly now, past one cluster of islands after another. It seemed they were sailing so closely she could reach out and touch them.

As they approached Sturgis Island, a small, remotely populated stretch of land, a rocky beach came into view. A weathered dock, an old warehouse and several ramshackle houseboats soon appeared out of the haze that still clung to the shoreline.

"You probably know that used to be an old fish processing plant," Vanessa said, pointing towards the dock. "I think it's called Sea farer's Cove. Several years ago after my parents added on the restaurant to the lodge, they worked out an agreement with the owners, Hank and Mary Anne Whitcomb, to purchase fresh seafood."

"I remember," Lowell said. "Hank and Mary Anne had a thriving operation. I'm not sure why their business went belly-up. Now that entire shoreline's nothing but a ghost town."

Unexpectedly an image of her father intruded on her thoughts and once again, guilt threatened to overcome her. *I should be looking for him right now—not sailing off to Iffleman Island,* she chided herself.

Yet tomorrow she'd have her chance for atonement. Tomorrow would make the difference. If the Fish and Wildlife agent knew something about her father, she would be right there to ask her own questions and not rely solely on Lowell.

They sailed on, island after island. At last they approached the west shore of Iffleman Island and set anchor in a quiet cove nestled between two jutting promontories. A sparsely wooded tract stretched up behind the rocky beach, and through a yawning gap in the forest, Vanessa spotted the main lodge of the old Boy Scout camp, surrounded by a ring of cabins.

"I hear the state has purchased the property with plans of turning it into a public campground," Lowell said, following her gaze. "And on the other side of the island, there are more new resorts and B&Bs than you can shake a stick at."

"I suppose change is good," she acknowledged, though not fully convinced. "It seems ages since my folks brought you and Andy here for the Eagle Scout weekend camp-out. Of course, I got to ride along too."

"You mean the time you nearly trashed my sleeping bag by emptying three cans of shaving cream inside?" One corner of his mouth turned up and his eyes sparkled mischievously, holding hers.

"You probably had it coming for one reason or another."

He chuckled. "Yep, I suppose so." He looked at his watch. "Hungry?"

"I'm ravenous."

"Good! Then let's go inside."

He opened the door that led into the cabin, gestured towards the booth in the galley and said, "Sit down. And close your eyes."

"Why?"

"Don't ask questions. Just do it."

She squeezed her eyes shut, cupping them with her hands. From across the galley, she could hear him opening a door, probably the refrigerator, and whistling an off-key tune. Then rustling. And more rustling. Next the door slammed shut, and a cupboard snapped open. Then came the sound of him popping a bottle cap.

"Okay, open!"

As she did, her hands flew to her mouth in amazement. There right before her was an opened picnic wicker basket, lined in a red-and-white checkered cloth. It was brimming with pocket bread sandwiches, succulent chunks of smoked salmon, an assortment of cheese and crackers, a tantalizing array of chilled tropical fruits, completed by petite fours decorated in a variety of pastel icings.

"I don't believe this! You got all this together in only one hour?" She blinked in amazement as he handed her a chilled long-stemmed glass filled with sparkling white wine.

"No, not exactly one hour," he answered, sending her a lop-sided grin. "I'm very organized. I plan ahead."

Deep inside new feelings stirred within her. It was apparent he'd gone to a great deal of effort putting together this feast. "This is wonderful, Lowell," she said, her voice softening. "Thank you."

"You're welcome." An awkward silence hung between them. "Actually, I made good use of that new little deli in town," he confessed, his tone turning business-like. "I doubt you've even had a chance to stop there since you've been back. But for now, what are we waiting for? Dig in!"

As they sat at the table eating, sunshine slanted through the porthole, catching a dust mote. The boat rocked gently. Somewhere off in the distance, the resonant blare of a tug boat horn wafted across the water. Between bites of pocket bread and sips of wine, they passed the next hour in quiet conversation, pausing to laugh at more shared remembrances or an occasional comment about Ruby and Clinton's endearing antics.

"When do you think their wedding will be?" Lowell asked, wiping his chin with an oversized paper napkin. "Or will they simply spare everyone the fuss by running off to elope?" He wadded up the napkin, tossed it alongside his empty plate, and clasped his hands behind his neck.

"Whoa," Vanessa said. "Don't be so presumptuous." She'd nearly forgotten how direct Lowell could sometimes be. "I'm sure they'll need more time before either of them speaks of marriage," she added cautiously. "At least, I know my uncle will. He still thinks he's a confirmed bachelor, even when he does admit his interest in Ruby."

After rinsing their dishes together in the tiny sink in the galley, they untied the dingy and rowed out to the beach. Then dragging the dingy onto the shore, they kicked off their shoes and started walking arm-in-arm. Farther out, white-tipped waves caught beams of sunlight. The gentle roar of the incoming tide mingled with the rhythm of their foot fall. Vanessa sighed. Peace. Peace everywhere. Yes, perhaps Lowell was right. She'd needed this reprieve, even if just for a few hours.

"Nessie." The sound of his voice sliced through her musing.

"Hmm?"

He stopped walking and turned to her. "Let's build a sandcastle again."

"What?" His words caught her off-guard, and she couldn't help giving a quick laugh. Was this Lowell talking? A tough, jaded cop suggesting they play in the sand?

"I know it may sound ludicrous, but it could be kind of fun," he went on. "The sand's moist enough and there are still several hours before high tide."

Something inside prodded her. Why not? Why not roll back the years and pretend they were kids again? Just like they'd been the last time they'd walked this beach—a happier time when Mom and Andy had been well and alive.

"All right. But what shall we use for sculpting tools? We didn't exactly come prepared for this, you know."

"There are always clam shells to use as scoopers. And look, I think I see an old discarded bucket up behind that log. It'll work perfect for the turrets."

For the remainder of the afternoon, they lost all track of time. Talking and laughing, they mounded and molded and carved away at the cool, damp sand. By sunset they'd finished. Their sandcastle stood broad and tall with its carefully crafted peaks and turrets and a wide encompassing mote.

In minutes the sea edged closer, first filling the mote, then claiming their castle as well. They watched transfixed, silhouetted against the mauve streaked sky, once again arm-in-arm.

Vanessa blinked back a tear. This was what life was all about, wasn't it? The rhythm of nature, playing out a ritual as old as time itself. Maybe good-byes didn't have to remain painful, at least, not forever. Perhaps there could be beauty and meaning to it all, no matter how bittersweet the parting.

She looked up at Lowell, her heart overflowing with love. Love not only for those in her life to whom she'd bidden good-bye, but a new love as well. Love for this boy-turned-man standing silently beside her.

And as he pulled her closer, his lips meeting hers in an urgent kiss, her heart could no longer close the door.

*****

"Dr. Paris! Where were you yesterday? I tried and tried to reach you!" Carmen's desperate voice came through on the other end of the office phone.

A bolt of fear shot through Vanessa. "What's wrong?" she asked. "Why didn't you leave a message with Ruby? I would've phoned you back the minute I got word!"

"I don't know. I don't know anything right now. I just need to talk to you."

It was clear now that the girl was sobbing, nearly hysterical.

"Please!" she exclaimed. When are you coming back?"

"Soon. In a couple of weeks."

"A couple of weeks! But I need you right now. I'll absolutely die if I have to wait that long!" Carmen's voice rose to a reedy pitch. "Everything's wrong! I'm bummed out! I don't know how I can go on. Oh, Dr. Paris, it's simply awful. Much too awful to talk about over the phone."

Vanessa's heart sank. What was she going to do? All morning, as she'd prepared to leave with Lowell for the mainland, her anticipation was skyrocketing. A thousand times over, she'd pictured herself, sitting next to him while the wildlife agent informed them he had hopeful news. But Carmen was impulsive, perhaps even suicidal. Vanessa couldn't afford to put her off. No, not even for an extra hour.

She inhaled slowly before answering. "All right, Carmen. You hang tight."

"You mean you'll come? You'll come right away?"

"Yes. I was planning a quick trip to Seattle this morning anyway. I should be there no later than nine. Meet me at the community resource counseling center on campus."

"All right, Dr. Paris. But just hurry. Please!"

"I will. I promise. See you at nine."

Less than twenty minutes later, Vanessa and Lowell were on their way. Now as they stood on the white washed deck of the ferry, Vanessa's mind churned.

Carmen. She couldn't have called at a worse time. But no one else on the counseling staff had managed to establish the rapport with

Carmen that Vanessa had. She simply couldn't stand by and do nothing.

As Lowell pulled her close, they peered across the Sound. The shoreline of Tawanya Island was still encased in the shroud of cool mist that had formed earlier as the sun warmed the tide-washed beach. In no time, the boat blasted its horn. The dock, small shops, and beach grew smaller, then inched out of sight.

"Thinking about Carmen?" he murmured.

"Uh-huh." On the way to the ferry landing, she'd told Lowell about the teenager's desperate call. "The poor girl's got a heap of problems," Vanessa reiterated with a sigh.

"Hmm, too bad."

"It's tragic, really. And unfortunately, Carmen's not alone. There are far too many kids standing in her shoes." As she leaned into him, she was acutely aware of his corded chest muscles beneath the thin fabric of his shirt. Swallowing hard, she tried to ignore the sweep of emotions washing over her. If he sensed how much she loved him, he might only retreat into himself further.

"Yes, good kids with bad problems," he said. "I see it every day myself. Sometimes in its rawest form."

She nodded wordlessly. Like an old refrain, the reminder marched through her mind. She could go about her work, shielded within the brick and ivy ambience of the sprawling university, plus the comfortable office where she conducted her counseling sessions. But Lowell's job cut to the very core of perhaps humanity's darkest side—the ghettos, the gangs, the inner-city violence. *Even death*.

Maybe she should regard Carmen's unexpected call as a timely reminder to get her sights back on track and forget all about him. Until yesterday, her life had no room for the entanglements of love, but her romantic interlude with him on Iffleman Island had changed that.

Yes, there was no denying, she wanted him for all time. Yet what good was a one-sided romance? And what kind of a future could she share with a man who continued to allow iron walls of silence to stand between them?

About an hour later, after arriving at the Fish and Wildlife headquarters, they went their separate ways. Lowell had insisted that Vanessa take his pickup to the university, a short distance away, while he met with the agent. "No point in hassling with bus connections when my truck's available," he'd told her, and gratefully she accepted.

At the counseling center, she was relieved to find Carmen sitting on a bench next to the courtyard that fronted the building. Leading the girl inside, unlocking the door to her office and offering her a chair, she listened attentively while Carmen cried and talked, then cried some more.

"So you see, Dr. Paris, it all boils down to this," she said, swiping at a tear with the sleeve of her T-shirt. "I finally gave Joey, my boyfriend, an ultimatum. Either he quit taking drugs once and for all and agree to get help, or we were through."

"Good for you, Carmen. So what was his answer?"

"He said he wasn't sure what was more important in his life. His drug habit or me."

After nearly another hour, Carmen finally admitted she was beginning to feel braver about her decision, thanking Vanessa for coming. Maybe, regardless of whether Joey and I stay together or not," she added, "I'll at least manage to talk him into joining our support group when you get back for good. Oh, please, Dr. Paris. Hurry back. You'll never know how much me and the kids miss you."

At the girl's words, Vanessa bit her lip. Her work was waiting for her, and Carmen was living testimony to that. But how could she return once again if she were still living in this dreadful limbo? Searching and waiting and not knowing. Squaring her shoulders, she attempted a smile. "I will, Carmen. I will be back soon."

Shortly before noon, as she approached the Fish and Wildlife headquarters, she spied Lowell pacing outside the front entrance. Every nerve in her body tensed as she swung into a parking space and braced herself for what he might say.

"How'd it go?" they exclaimed in unison after he'd climbed into the passenger side of the pickup. Their ensuing laughter eased the tension that was growing more palpable with each passing moment.

Still parked, allowing the engine to idle. she was the first to speak next. "All right. You first." She shifted beneath his gaze, her heart racing like a herd of thundering elephants.

"The agent I spoke with is Ralph Morrison." Lowell's tone was guarded. "Good thing the sheriff put me onto him, because I think he's the right man to help us."

"Oh?"

"That's right. Morrison told me there has been illegal killing and trafficking of wildlife in the islands these past several months."

"What kind of killing?"

"Sea otters. The poachers are catching them farther out in the ocean, near Neah Bay, them hauling them back to the islands and stashing the carcasses in some unknown place. Morrison's been working undercover, trying to get to the bottom of it."

"But I don't understand," Vanessa stammered. "What does this have to do with my father?" She continued to allow the motor to idle, her hands fixed stiffly on the steering wheel while she gave no thought to driving away.

Morrison has evidence that Eldon may have gotten mixed up in this, but he couldn't tell me everything. Part of what he knows is protected information."

No! That's ludicrous!" Her face flamed with disbelief and indignation. "Dad would never get involved in anything illegal, especially destroying the wildlife he loves!"

"It doesn't make sense to me either. But I respect Morrison's input. Normally, I hear, he doesn't miss a beat. Right now he's organizing a fifty-man task force to get to the bottom of this. They're hoping to pull off a bust as soon as possible."

"So what now?" she asked, nearly choking on her words. "Is there any more either of us can do?" She squeezed her hands together till her knuckles turned white.

"You must stick close to the lodge, you and Clinton both. As for me, I'm going to get involved in some undercover work myself."

"What do you mean?"

"Morrison says the poachers are posing as fishing guides. I plan to conduct my surveillance by signing up for as many excursions as possible."

"No, Lowell! Don't! Please!" Vanessa's voice broke as tears blurred her vision. "Wildlife busts can be as lethal as drug busts! I've heard and read all about it. Some agents have been shot, even strangled!"

He tossed her an impatient look, his eyes dark. "Nessie. Listen up. Don't get female on me, not at a time like this."

"I'm not! Just because I asked you to help me look for Dad doesn't mean I wanted you to put your safety in jeopardy. I never dreamed things would get this complicated.

"That's life." He lifted one shoulder. "Sometimes life *is* complicated."

"But you just said there's a fifty-man task force. Let them do it." She locked her gaze with his. "Why you? Why must *you* get involved too?"

Chapter Eight

In the week that followed, Vanessa moved methodically through each day, her thoughts frozen in terror. Terror for Lowell, who'd refused to listen to her pleas. Terror for her father, who'd been missing for nearly three weeks. Regardless of what Ralph Morrison had said, she refused to believe Eldon had been linked with the sea otter killings.

Yet somehow, life ticked by, and Vanessa repeatedly found herself asking how. How could the sun and moon keep rising and setting? The tides ebb and flow? How could the world go on as if Eldon Paris had never existed?

True, his name was always on the lips of his old cronies, the small population of islanders who'd known him for nearly half a century. Aside from that, the pulse beat on Tawanya Island continued in its customary fashion: unhurried, peaceful. It seemed unfathomable that there could be illegal operations in progress somewhere close by.

Worse, Lowell was putting himself at risk as well. Clinton had been more than willing to go along with his plan, allowing him extra time off for his undercover surveillance. Her uncle's ready cooperation only weakened her efforts to try to persuade Lowell to change his mind. Every morning as Vanessa watched him drive away, she had no choice but to face the possibility that now he, too, walked that thin line of danger.

And now she was more fearful than ever. Yet why? she wondered. Hadn't she succeeded in overcoming her fears? Hadn't Lowell unknowingly shown her how when he'd insisted they linger on the beach a little while longer, watching the sea wash away their sandcastle?

No, perhaps she still hadn't found complete peace, she finally decided. At least, not when it came to her fear of losing Lowell. Yet time and time again she found herself daydreaming of their future together as man and wife, reuniting after their respectively busy days, sharing hearth and home, making wonderful, passionate love.

But could this ever come to fruition—especially when Lowell continued to battle with his own private demons? The obstacles that loomed between them, like gloomy lurking shadows, seemed to be growing larger with each passing day. To keep from going altogether crazy, she threw herself into helping Clinton and Ruby. The office had to be manned constantly, the housekeeping and restaurant operations maintained, and above all, the guests kept happy. Thankfully, the daily routine consumed her.

Saturday morning in the basement laundry room while Vanessa sorted the day's laundry, the hum of the washing machines and dryers lulled her anxious thoughts.

She heard footsteps on the stairs and looked up. The housekeepers were due to arrive anytime now, yet a hunch told her the unannounced visitor was someone else.

Her hunch was right.

Ruby waltzed into the room, wearing a lop-sided grin. "I thought you took the day off," Vanessa exclaimed. "And don't tell me you can't stay away. Especially not after all the time you've put in around here. But wait a minute . . . Why are you smiling like that?"

"Clinton is taking me to the mainland for the annual classical musical festival—that is, if you think you can get along without him for a few hours."

Vanessa smiled back, sending Ruby a conspiratorial look. "Get along without him? You bet I can! You tell my uncle he'd better plan on making a day of it. I don't want to see the whites of his eyes—nor yours—any time before midnight!" As she gave the towel she was holding a swift shake, the fragrance of detergent and fabric softener wafted about them.

Ruby's face brightened even more. "The *whole* day? Do you think Clinton will agree to that? Who will take care of Toby?"

"Don't worry. I will." It was the least she could do. And if Ruby had managed to interest Clinton in classical music, then she must certainly be gaining ground.

How lucky Ruby was to be experiencing *an uncomplicated romance,* Vanessa mused

"Ruby?"

"Yes, child?"

"May I talk to you for a moment?"

"Why of course. What is it?" Ruby perched herself on the bar stool next to the folding table and linked her hands together in her lap.

"I don't know exactly how to say this, but I think I'm falling in love with Lowell. Why at a time like this, I'll never know."

"Aw, yes. I'm not surprised. I've seen it coming. I've seen it in your eyes." Ruby reached out to touch her arm. "But he hasn't come around yet, has he? He still hasn't told you what's troubling him."

"No, I'm afraid not."

Ruby nodded, understanding flooding her eyes. "Such a pity. Lowell's such a good-looking, honorable young man. I hate to see him suffering this way."

Vanessa sucked in a deep draft of air. "Are you sure you can't tell me what he said? If I only knew, then maybe, somehow, I could help him."

"I must keep my word to him." Ruby hesitated, pursing her lips. "I do believe there still is hope."

"How?"

"I have a feeling that one of these days—I pray soon—the right moment will come. But you must be patient, Vanessa. You of all people should know that healing takes time."

"Yes." Vanessa heaved a weary sigh. "But time is running out for both of us. Lowell and I'll be leaving soon, in only about a week."

"I know."

Vanessa bit her lip as she folded a clean towel and placed it on top of a stack of others. "Maybe I'm only kidding myself. Maybe when I first thought I was falling for Lowell, I was only trying to run away from my problems. Maybe we both were."

She described their afternoon on Iffleman Island, how they'd built the sandcastle, then watched it wash out to sea. "It was so beautiful, Ruby. More beautiful than anything I can ever describe. That's what love is all about, isn't it? Sharing something beautiful. Something so beautiful you feel as if you're about to burst inside."

"Yes, that and much more," Ruby replied breaking into a slow smile, her eyes bright with years of wisdom. "But if your feelings for Lowell are truly as you say, then your heart will know. Listen to your heart. It won't steer you wrong."

Vanessa straightened, suddenly remembering the look on Ruby's face only moments earlier. Was Ruby in love with Clinton? Could that be what her radiance had meant? At any rate, she intended to rain on Ruby's picnic by talking about her own problems.

"I'm sorry, Ruby," she said softly. "I didn't mean to get side-tracked. I'm really happy about you and my uncle. Now just tell me what I need to do for Toby and then be on your way. I hope the day turns out perfect for both of you."

Beaming once again, the older women ticked off her instructions on her fingers, from exactly how to serve Toby the specialty dog food she was buying for him at the feed store to which trails he preferred for chasing grey digger squirrels. "Gosh!" Vanessa laughed despite herself. "I think you're spoiling that dog worse than Lowell is."

"Now that's debatable!" Ruby fluttered one hand in the air and turned on her heel to leave. "See you later, my dear. I'll tell you all about the music festival tomorrow."

"Yes, you do that," Vanessa called after her. "And be sure to bring back a program."

"Speaking of Toby, I couldn't help overhearing." No sooner had Ruby left, Lawrence appeared at the back door, clasping a worn trowel.

His bulky form nearly eclipsed the rectangle of sunlight that streamed through the open door.

"Why, good morning, Lawrence." Vanessa's face flushed. Had Lawrence heard them talking about Lowell too? "What is it you want to know about Toby?"

The corners of his eyes crinkled in a good-natured squint. "I just wanted to say I sure hope whoever's taking care of that mutt can keep him from digging anymore in my flower beds!"

Vanessa reached for a pile of bath towels, still warm from the dryer. "Yes, I'm dreadfully sorry. I'll keep Toby in the fenced yard right off the family quarters. There's nothing there he can harm."

"Well now, I suppose we shouldn't be too hard on the little feller," the gardener relented, breaking into a wider smile. "Maybe he's just discovering what it's like to be a land-lubber again." He ran his tongue over his lower lip. "Any news yet about your father?"

"No, I'm afraid not." She stopped abruptly, least she say something about Lowell's undercover surveillance. He'd cautioned her that no one other than Clinton must know.

"I'm a-prayin' for him," Lawrence put in, scratching the gray fringe of his balding head. "I swear, Miss Paris, once the search parties have been called off, the only thing left a body can do is pray. And you know what they say about the Lord helping those who help themselves."

"Yes. Thanks again for your concern." Vanessa paused to regard him thoughtfully. "By the way, Lawrence, was that you operating the Boston Whaler that almost collided with Lowell's sailboat last week?"

Fear sprang to the gardener's dark brown eyes. "Oh, yes um. I'm so sorry about that, Miss Paris, really I am. Me and my buddies, we'd been out having a good time on the water and Bart, who owns the boat, asked me if I'd like to try my hand at driving it. I'm sort of a land-lubber, you see, just like this here mutt we were talking about."

"Well, you nearly ran us down. You must be more careful. Especially when the waterways are so jammed with holiday boaters."

He hung his head repentantly. "Oh, yes um. That'll never happen again. I swear. Truth is, I realized the danger myself and signed up at the marina for a water-safety course."

"That's good. Very good."

The older man tipped his brimmed straw hat and motioned outside. "I gotta get going, Miss Paris. Gonna be a scorcher of a day, I'm afraid. Time to set up the sprinklers."

She gave a forced smile, hoping she hadn't come on too harshly. Her conversation with Ruby about Lowell moments earlier had unnerved her, leaving her tense and edgy.

"See you later, Lawrence. And don't stay out in the sun too long."

"Don't worry. I won't."

After he'd disappeared, she refocused her energies to the inane task of folding the rest of the towels. Yet Lowell's image kept hovering on the fringes of her mind. So far all week, she hadn't talked to him more than a total of thirty minutes. She yearned to be with him, to share that something beautiful she and Ruby had contemplated together. Yet she was seeing less and less of him, and the longer he stayed away, it felt as if he were slipping out of her reach forever.

*****

Next evening, after hauling in the crab pots, Vanessa sat cross-legged on the dock watching the last glimmers of sunlight reflecting off the water. Dusk was gathering, like plush velvet, splashing shadows of indigo and slate against the distant shoreline. To the west, not far from a waxing moon, the evening star glittered, one solitary jewel poking through the heavens. A gull flapped, coming to land only inches from her feet. It cocked its head and blinked a beady eye inquisitively in her direction.

Vanessa felt no urgency to leave. She needed to memorize every color and texture, fix in her mind the sights, smells, and sounds that made up this tapestry of loveliness. Already the days were growing noticeably shorter, a gnawing reminder that the summer was more than half over.

"Good evenin', miss." A fisherman, who'd just finished tying up on the far end of the pier, sauntered by and greeted her.

"Any luck?" Vanessa asked politely.

"Nope, not this time," he answered with a wan smile. "Maybe tomorrow."

She watched his retreating figure grow smaller until it had faded into the shadows. On the shore near pilings of driftwood, two campfires flickered. The voices of parents and young children carried across the water while the faint smells of charbroiled hamburgers drifted her way.

Suddenly she spied Lowell striding down the dock, carrying a grocery bag.

Something caught at the base of her throat. Without a doubt, he was returning to the sailboat again after another long day on the Sound. How she'd missed him this past week.

Wearing cut-offs and a white polo shirt, he drew nearer. "Hungry?" he asked, sending her a disarming smile. "I just came from the market in town on my way home from Barachman Bay. "The fishing was lousy," he added, as if for the benefit of anyone who might be eavesdropping. The intensity in his eyes belied his casual voice.

"Well, I guess it has been a while since the last time I ate," she admitted.

"Good. I bought a loaf of French bread, a bottle of wine, fresh crab and T-bone steaks," he went on. "I decided that since it's such a terrific evening, I'd barbecue on the deck."

She studied him a long moment. The sun had deepened his already bronze tan. Tiny lines of fatigue fanned out from the corners of his eyes.

Smiling again, he pulled her to her feet, and for an immeasurable moment, he didn't let go.

A short time later after he'd broiled the steaks on the deck of Sea Breeze, he brought them inside and set them on the counter in the galley.

"So what have you learned?" she asked in a hushed voice as she finished tossing a green salad with vinegar and oil.

He popped the cork on the bottle of wine and poured, first her glass, then his. "Nothing substantial, but it's still early. So far, I've only gone out on four excursions. There's at least a half a dozen more guide services here on Tawanya Island and each one runs several times a week."

For the next hour they shared small talk and laughter—eyes meeting eyes, hands touching hands.

The scenario was disturbingly familiar. Here she was sitting face-to-face with him again, sipping fine wine, and listening to soft jazz streaming from his phone. The intimacy was becoming more overpowering with each passing moment.

Quickly she got to her feet. "Thanks for a delicious dinner, but it's time for me go. Morning will come early for both of us."

"Yes, it will." He reached out and clasped her shoulders, facing her squarely. "I've missed you this week, Nessie. I've missed you terribly."

"I've missed you too."

In the dim light of the cabin, she could detect the play of emotions flickering across his face: caution, longing, fear, indecision. The lonely sound of a fog horn wafted across the bay.

Urging her against his broad chest, he threaded his fingers through her hair, causing shivers of delight to course through her.

"Ah, Nessie," he murmured. She could feel his heart thudding. "I don't like being away from you like this. I don't want you to go." Hungrily his lips played against hers.

Abandoning all heed, she kissed him back. Their tongues touched, darted intimately. She could never get enough of him. Never.

Sometime later, she couldn't be sure when, their embrace ended.

"Oh, Lowell, I love you so much," she murmured, resting her head on his shoulder, reluctant to break the contact. "I wasn't sure about anything before, but now I am."

A strained silence followed. As her eyes riveted on him, she saw the color drain from his face.

"Sit down," he said thickly.

She did. He positioned himself next to her on the daybed.

"I think we'd better talk." A shadow passed over his face.

"What is it?" she asked in a small voice.

"When you first came back home, I told you I wasn't in any state of mind for a relationship," he began haltingly. "I do care about you, Nessie. I care deeply, but sometimes caring isn't enough."

Her stomach twisted as she waited for him to continue. "As you know, I took leave from the L.A. police force in hopes of working through some things." He wedged his folded hands between his knees and stared down at the floor.

"Yes, go on."

"One day not long before I left, my partner and I were on patrol together. I call Garrett my partner, but he was more than just that. He was a friend too. Garrett Vanaken and his wife Muriel had three wonderful little boys."

She lifted her gaze to the brass-framed photo across from them and pointed. "That picture . . . are those children their sons?"

"Uh-huh." He swallowed hard. "Garrett and Muriel often asked me over for Sunday dinners and trips to the zoo with the boys. Next to yours, maybe, I've never seen such a happy, close-knit family. When Garrett and I weren't spending time with them, sometimes we went off together for a day of sailing. He owned a boat a lot like this one."

"So what happened?"

"Garrett was new on the force, just a couple of years out of the academy. That day we were on duty together, we spotted a pick-up with a burned-out tail light on the interstate. Though the driver pulled over as soon as he saw our flashing lights, it turned out he had no intentions of cooperating. Garrett approached him to issue a warning while I stayed back in the patrol car to radio in." His voice broke. "I should've covered Garrett . . . but I got careless . . . I figured a broken tail-light was no big deal. We both did." He put his head in his hands, unable to go on.

"And? Then what?"

He looked up again and drew in a steadying breath. "The driver of the pick-up had a gun, lots of cocaine, and a history of drug charges. He undoubtedly panicked, figuring he'd get caught. The guy fired twice. Garrett died on the scene. Another cop who happened to be driving by witnessed what happened and pulled over. We managed to get the guy on the ground, spread eagle, and then hand-cuffed him."

"Oh, no! How tragic," she breathed. "I'm sorry, Lowell. So sorry." She longed to reach out and touch him, but something held her back.

"Yes, it was more than tragic." The angles of his face hardened as he carefully avoided her gaze. "It was a stinkin' injustice. I should've been the one gunned down, Vanessa. Not Garrett. Not a dedicated family man with a wife and three kids. I made a bad call. I let myself get sloppy. I should've covered his rear, but I didn't."

"Oh, Lowell, you mustn't beat yourself up that way. That kind of guilt can only be counterproductive. You mustn't let it destroy you."

He shook his head. "*I* was the officer with the most experience. I should've known better." He faltered. "Besides, I know what it's like to grow up without a dad. I know what that can do to a family. If anyone should've been killed, it was me, not Garrett. I don't deserve to be happy. I don't deserve to marry and have a family of my own."

"You're wrong. Terribly wrong. You're a good man, Lowell. You *do* deserve happiness. And the accident. That's all it was, you know. Simply a tragic accident. You must believe that."

"No." He paused, squaring his jaw.

"So that's why you also blamed yourself when my father disappeared?" she asked, filling in the missing pieces. "You were reliving your guilt because you felt responsible for what happened to Dad?"

"Yes, that, plus the obvious fact that there's a job to do. Once a cop, always a cop." He dropped his gaze. His declaration fell like a death sentence as he added, "I can't give you my love, Vanessa, but I will give you my word. I'll do whatever it takes. I'll keeping looking for Eldon right till it's time for me to go back to L.A."

Chapter Nine

The next few days, Vanessa lived and breathed and moved in a vacuum. Lowell was busy again, scoping out one fishing excursion after the next, and like before, they saw very little of each other.

She ached for him, for the pain and suffering he'd buried deep inside. Over the past few weeks back here on the island, her own heart had begun to heal. She knew now that her mother and brother would always live on in her memory, and no one could ever take that away from her. The healing would go on, and because of that, she was ready to reach out again. She could love and be loved and not fear the consequences.

But Lowell had been dealt a double-edged blow. He was not only grieving for Garrett, he was also dealing with guilt.

The guilt Vaness had experienced the day she'd gone sailing with Lowell, instead of looking for her father, had been one grain of sand in an invisible hour glass. Lowell's guilt encompassed billions of others. Ruby was right. His healing would require time. But how much longer would it take for the sands in the hour glass to empty? And how much longer could she wait for him to change his mind about loving her, especially now that he'd sworn it could never be.

Wednesday morning, a letter in a plain white envelope arrived addressed to Vanessa. Tearing it open, not bothering to grab the ivory letter opener she'd left on the office desk, she began reading the type-written message:

This an anonymous note to inform you of your father's whereabouts. He is alive in a deserted houseboat near the old fishing packing plant at Seafarer's Cove on Sturgis Island. It's time for you to come for him. I assure you, I seek no ransom. By the time you receive this, I'll be well on my way out of the country anyway.

She stuffed the letter into her breast pocket, her hands trembling. Her father was alive! Alive and close by! He'd been the entire time!

Without warning, fear eclipsed her joy. There were still too many unanswered questions. What if this was a set-up? Could this be a trap to kidnap her too?

The fear twisted deeper. She rushed to the front window, peering out at the parking lot. *Lowell! Please be here!*

Yet his truck was gone again and so was he. Gone for the entire day, most likely, miles away on the Sound for another guided fishing trip, perhaps even as far as the ocean itself.

Gathering her wits, she knew there was no time to lose! So what if Lowell had warned her to stay close by the lodge? That was ridiculous! How could she stay put now? Especially when Dad's life was still hanging in the balance?

She decided to leave a note for Ruby and Clinton, phone a message to the sheriff's department, and be on her way.

In no time, expertly maneuvering Clinton's motor boat, she sped into the bay towards Sturgis Island. The boat pitched across the Sound, jolting her like a bucking bronco. Rain pounded against the top of the cabin. She could feel the counter-force of the wind, hear its muffled roar, see the rising swells of gray-green water undulating before her. The wind had risen to nearly 28 knots.

Shivering, more out of fear than the penetrating chill, she considered for a moment. Maybe she should turn back. Wait till the weather cleared. But just as quickly as the temptation had surfaced, she pulled her thoughts back into focus. She mustn't let the storm stop her. There was no choice but to stay on course.

Half an hour later she was nearly there. The downpour continued, slanting before her in glistening silvery sheets, nearly obscuring her vision. Then, through the mist, the shoreline appeared, a gray rocky beach where the water and the land seemed to merge into one.

She tied the boat, then hurried down the weathered dock. It swayed beneath her. Large raindrops spilled off the wide brim of her vinyl rain hat. Biting spray of saltwater stung her face. A seagull shrieked from overhead, then landed atop another small boat docked close by.

At the end of the dock, she paused to scan the long row of boathouses. There must've been close to a dozen. Where should she start looking? The front window of the nearest houseboat was boarded. So were the others. There was no smoke curling from any chimney. No firewood stacked on any porch. No sign of activity anywhere. Fresh fear seeped through her. What did this mean? Had the letter been intended as a red herring?

Shoving the thought aside, thinking only of her father, she began pounding the door of the first houseboat. Silence was her only answer. She continued, houseboat after houseboat, her chest growing tighter by the second. *Dad! Where are you? Please, God! Please don't let this be a hoax! Please let my father be here!*

Peering straight ahead, she made a quick count. Only three houseboats left. At the next, she rapped even more loudly than before, then caught the muted sound of someone inside coughing. Without a moment's hesitation, she slammed her shoulder against the door's rough surface, amazed at how easily it flung open.

Her heart thudded wildly as her gaze swept the narrow room. Directly across from her was an old free-standing Franklin stove, though it appeared it hadn't been used in years. There was no furniture except a dilapidated Formica-covered table and a wooden bench. A musty damp smell assaulted her nostrils.

"Who's here?" she called in a small voice. More coughing coming from somewhere in the back. She pressed forward and found herself inside a dark passageway that led to a small room. Entering cautiously, she waited for her eyes to adjust to the dimness. A frigid draft washed over her.

"Vanessa," came a weak cry, then more coughing.

"Dad! Oh, Dad!" She gasped, her head whirling. He was tied to a chair, hands bound behind him.

"Hold on!" she cried. "I'll help you. I'll get you free."

A yawning door, dangling half-suspended from rusty hinges, slammed open and shut. At the top was a broken window. Her eyes darted about frantically, coming to rest on the shards of glass that lay scattered at the foot of the door.

She grasped the closest shard, then attempted to cut through the cord. It seemed to take forever. At last, severed, it snapped free. "We've got to get help! We've got to get you to a hospital," she said in a frenzy.

Eldon appeared several pounds thinner. His face was flushed with fever, his eyes dull. His voice broke as his warm tears moistened her cheek. "Vanessa, my kitten . . . I thought I'd never see you again." His words were dissolved by more coughing until at last he managed, "This cough . . . it's tearing my lungs apart."

"I know, Dad. Clinton's boat is outside. I'll go for help." She darted a nervous look through the half opened back door

"I've had food. And a little water. But I'm so sick."

"Who kidnapped you? Who would ever do something so outrageous as this?"

Before he could answer, the sound of thudding footsteps on the front porch sliced through her thoughts. The footsteps fell louder as the intruders gained entry and stormed into the houseboat. Vanessa froze, standing rooted to the ground.

Three men loomed before her—but the images of the outer two faded as her focus sharpened on the one in the middle. *Lowell!*

"Vanessa!" His eyes widened. "So you *did* come. I saw Clinton's boat at the dock. I thought it might be him instead."

"Did the sheriff tell you about the anonymous letter?" Her heart was racing, her breathing so rapid she feared she might pass out.

"Yes. And there's more to the story. But right now we must take care of your father."

Lowell and the other two men lowered Eldon onto the floor, covered him with a gray wool blanket and secured an oxygen mask in place. Judging from the insignias on their jackets, they were officers from the Fish and Wildlife department.

"Hold on, Eldon. You'll feel better in a minute," Lowell murmured with a firmness that was at the same time so gentle it made her heart turn over. "We've radioed for the medevac copter. It should arrive any minute now."

Several more agents rushed in, clustered about. Reinforcements, Vanessa assumed.

Jerking her attention back to her father, so wracked with cough, so wonderfully dear, she hunkered down alongside him. "Your heart pills, Dad. How did you ever get along without them?"

He shook his head weakly, squeezing his eyes shut. "I didn't have to. I had the pills right here."

"But how did you get them?"

"Shh!" Lowell broke in. "Don't tire him. I'll brief you later."

She slanted Lowell a quick look, a look filled with desperation and unspoken questions not only about her father, but the two of them as well.

Wordlessly he matched it, holding her gaze. The tension spiraled between them, transparent, invisible—and yet so undeniable.

The drone of a helicopter grew louder, shattering the spell. The noise mixed with the static of the officers' radios.

In seconds a flight nurse and an emergency medical technician were carrying Eldon Paris on a stretcher to the waiting copter while the other agents filed back to two patrol boats at the dock. Vanessa strode next to her father, keenly aware of Lowell's presence behind them.

"Don't worry, Dad," she said above the din of the copter and the agents' raised voices. "You're in good hands. You're going to be fine." Choking back her escalating dread, she bent over and kissed him on the forehead. His skin felt dry and hot. He appeared weak and frail.

Oh dear God, please help him pull through.

Her father smiled tremulously back at her with trusting gray eyes, though Vanessa sensed the fear his look masked. "Yes, kitten. Go home now. I'll be quite fine."

*****

"Uncle Clint! Uncle Clint!" Vanessa clamored into the family living quarters. "I found Dad! Lowell and the wildlife agents—"

Clinton dug into his hip pocket for his car keys and jangled them nervously. "Yes, yes, I know. I'm still pinching myself to believe it's true. Lowell called about a half an hour ago. How did Eldon look? How sick is he?"

She told him about the cough and fever and what little she knew about the heart pills. "It's scary," she added, raking her hands through her wind-tangled hair. "All along I was sick with worry about his heart condition, and now there's the possibility of pneumonia too. I'm not sure how much stamina Dad has to fight it, after being shut up in that musty old house boat without any heat."

"Lowell wants us to meet him in town at the sheriff's right away."

"But what about Dad? I was planning to catch the next ferry! Hurry to the hospital as soon as possible!"

"I know, kiddo. I'm anxious to get going too. But I'm sure the doctors can't tell us nothin' about Eldon till after they've run all their confounded tests, and it really is important we hear what the sheriff has to say." Her uncle shot her a stern look. "By the way, Lowell also said he tried to talk you into letting him follow you back here in one of the patrol boats, but you insisted on coming alone. He was worried the storm would pick up again. He was worried about your safety."

She lifted her chin, hoping he couldn't read on her face the anguish she felt deep inside. "After everything I went through to find Dad, getting back was the easy part." Those moments following her dad's departure, moments wrought with a kaleidoscope of mixed emotions, she would have so welcomed the feeling of Lowell's strong, masculine arms wrapped around her. But they were through now. Dad had been found. The mission was over.

Clinton shrugged quickly into his denim jacket, then motioned towards the door. "Well, you're here now and that's all that matters. Come on. There's not a minute to waste."

*****

"The wildlife authorities have almost finished filling out their reports downstairs," the sheriff began. "Thank you for coming."

"You're welcome, Sheriff Morton," Vanessa replied shakily. She and Clinton were sitting side-by-side facing him at a long narrow table in a conference room.

"Officer Maxwell said he'd be up in a minute," the sheriff continued. "In the meantime, I promised him I'd explain what we now know about your father."

Vanessa twisted the strap of her handbag, her nerves raw, dangerously on edge. "Yes, we need some answers. Who was keeping Dad in the deserted houseboat? Who would ever want to hold him captive?"

The sheriff leaned back and clasped his hands behind his head. "As you've already know, there's been a network of sea otter poachers here in the San Juans. Though most of the offenders on the other islands have already been caught—most were posing as fishing guides—there was evidence of activity still going on right here." He cleared his throat. "Earlier last month, Eldon Paris came across a stash of carcasses at the old lockers near the fish packing plant. At the same time he also came across his friend, Matt Redding, who was not only responsible for the poaching, but was also turning over huge profits on the European black market."

"Matt!" Shock waves crashed over her.

"Jumpin' jack rabbits!" Clinton put in. "*Matt Redding* was the guilty one?"

Sheriff Morton nodded, peering at them over his reading glasses, then went on. "At the bait shop the next day, the morning Mr. Paris disappeared, he and Redding had a bitter quarrel. Your father tried to convince Redding to turn himself in, but Redding refused. Later Redding got scared. He was afraid Mr. Paris would report him, so Redding caught up with him on The Lady Luck, knocked him out, and dragged him onto his own boat."

The color drained from Clinton's face. "So what's happened to Matt? Has he been arrested?"

"Yes, in violation of the Marine Mammal Protection act. He's been taken to the county jail in Seattle where he's awaiting arraignment. A few days ago Officer Maxwell discovered the lockers, too, and had good reason to believe Redding was responsible. That's when Maxwell tightened his surveillance, waiting to get the goods on Redding." The chair creaked as he shifted his weight. "His opportunity came early this morning, barely at the crack of dawn. While Redding and one of his dealers were exchanging hides for big bucks, the officers moved in and busted them. Without a shootout, mind you. Redding had planned to rake in his final profits, then money in hand, split for Canada."

"Oh no," Vanessa pressed an open hand against her chest. "I can't believe this. I knew Matt needed money for Fern's nursing home costs, but I never dreamed he'd go to this end." Her heart went out to him. Despite his wrong-doing, he was still a good man. He could have killed her father, but he didn't.

"Moments after the bust," the sheriff continued, "Redding confessed, giving every detail. He was the one, Ms. Paris, who'd sent you the letter. He wanted to make sure your father was discovered and got the help he needed."

"And I bet Matt was the one who brought my father his heart pills, and kept him supplied with food and water," she surmised out loud. "Surely after all this time, Dad couldn't have survived otherwise."

"That's right."

Vanessa momentarily shut her eyes, then opened them slowly. She felt spent. Bone weary. And knowing the details of Lowell's participation in the sting only added to her anxiety. "Are the lockers at the old fish packing plant still working after all these years?" she asked in amazement.

"Yes. Redding took care of the necessary repairs, reactivated the generators, and got the lockers operating again. He figured for a time, at least, he was sitting pretty."

"Lowell should certainly be congratulated," Clinton said heartily. "An operation like that couldn't have been easy to pull off."

"Yes, I agree," the sheriff answered. "The man does deserve our congratulations. He mingles well with the locals. Gains their confidence. In all my years on the department, I've never seen such professional undercover work."

The door to the outside opened suddenly and a blast of air swooshed through.

"Sorry those reports took me so long." Lowell's voice grew louder.

"Not a problem," the sheriff answered. "Come take a seat. I've just finished telling these folks the story. I think we've covered all the bases."

As Vanessa felt Lowell's arm brush hers, another rush of longing seized her. Quickly she forced it away.

"Thanks, sheriff," Lowell said. He sat down in the empty chair alongside her, only inches away. Vanessa's heart was hammering so loudly, she swore everyone else could hear too.

"Any word yet about Eldon?" Lowell asked, his gaze sweeping from first Clinton to Vanessa.

"No, not yet," Clinton answered. "We're heading over to the mainland in just a little while."

Lowell leveled his gaze on her, searching her face. "How're you holding up, Nessie?"

"All right." She could tell by the look in his eyes he didn't believe her. "And now if you'll excuse us," she added stiffly as she pushed herself to her feet, "Clinton and I must be on our way." In the distance, a siren wailed.

He rose too and placed a restraining hand on her shoulder. "Before you go, Vanessa, I'd like to have a word with you." His eyes hardened as he added, "Alone."

Chapter Ten

"What is it?" Vanessa asked tightly. Lowell had led her across the hall to a smaller office, the one the sheriff had been allowing him to use these past several days. She sat on a folding chair while he paced back and forth, arms crossed.

"I've come to an important decision, Vanessa. I've already explained to Clinton when I phoned him earlier."

"What is it?"

"I'm leaving tonight."

"*Tonight?*" She felt as if someone had pierced her chest with an arrow.

"Uh-huh, but not back to L.A."

"Then where *are* you going?"

"A while ago, just before Morrison left to go back to the Fish and Wildlife headquarters, he offered me a job with the department. I accepted."

"I see." Her words caught in her throat. "Well. Congratulations."

He stopped pacing. "First thing in the morning I'm calling my boss on the L.A. force and my landlord too. My rent's paid up till the end of the month. Morrison's agreed to give me a long weekend off then so I can drive back and take care of loose ends."

"Yes. Yes, of course."

He reached for her hands and pulled her to her feet. "I just wanted you to know, I believe this is the right move for me. Coming back to the Northwest has put me in touch with my roots, helped me define who I really am. I don't want to let go of that."

"But why must you leave *tonight?*" Her thoughts ricocheted between wanting to prolong their inevitable good-byes and doing so as quickly as possible.

"Morrison needs me immediately. He's offered me his guest house till I can find a place to live. The department's been short-handed far too long." His gaze flitted down to her lips, then rested again with her eyes.

"Well then." She swallowed against the sting of tears. "I guess the time has come a little earlier than we'd planned."

He shrugged. "What difference does a few days make?"

"Right. What difference?"

"Later tonight after I get settled, I'll call the hospital and ask about Eldon. And as soon as they'll let me see him, I plan to do that too." His voice was heavy with regret. "I need to tell him I'm sorry. If I'd known what had been going on before he left, there's no way I would've overslept that morning."

"You'll have your chance," she forced herself to reply airily. *But would he? What if Dad took a turn for the worse and died before Lowell could see him?*

"Good luck with the teen support group," he added thickly," and everything else you do in the future too." He gave a wry smile. "All those times I've teased you about your causes, I do hope you realize I *was* only teasing."

"Yes. I knew that." She averted her gaze.

He reached out and turned her chin till she had no choice but to meet his eyes again. The heat in his hand seemed to sear right through her. "Good-bye, Nessie."

"Good-bye, Lowell."

He brushed her lips with a soft, fleeting kiss, then escorted her back to the conference room where Clinton was waiting.

*****

"The charge nurse says Dad's in x-ray," Vanessa told her uncle as she slumped down in the white leather couch across from him in the waiting room on the fifth floor of the hospital. "They're doing chest x-rays, then an x-ray of his heart."

"So the doc suspects pneumonia? And more heart problems too?" Clinton asked shakily.

"They're already fairly certain about the pneumonia. Dr. Conford, his physician, says Dad's chest is congested. The x-ray of Dad's heart, an echocardiogram, is to rule out any not so obvious problems." She paused to dab a wadded-up tissue at the corner of her eyes. "They want to make sure the fluid on his lungs is not an indication of a weakened heart. And if the fluid backs up, Dad could have even worse problems." Two nurses in pale green surgical scrubs hurried by.

"But Eldon stayed right on schedule taking his heart pills. Wouldn't that have helped?"

"Hopefully yes." Through Vanessa struggled to sound as controlled as possible for her uncle's sake, inside she was crumbling into a million pieces. What an emotional roller-coaster the day had been. The joy over Dad's rescue, only to be complicated by the reality he could still die.

And now—she choked back a sob—Lowell's bittersweet farewell. He said he'd be calling the hospital, perhaps stopping by. She prayed that when he did, she would no longer be there. The prospect of seeing him again nearly ripped her in two. They'd already said their good-byes. She simply couldn't bear it one more time.

Later after Eldon had returned from the radiology department back to his hospital room, he drifted into a deep sleep. The x-ray had shown an advanced case of pneumonia, and the heart monitor now indicated an irregular rhythm. Only moments earlier, the charge nurse had informed them a cardiologist would be evaluating the echocardiogram within the next hour.

Clinton ran his hand across a gray-white stubble of beard. "Did you bring your cell phone, Vanessa? I need to get in touch with Ruby. I'm sure everyone back home is on pins and needles, wantin' to know." He gave a wry grin. "There are also a few things I want to tell Ruby in private."

"Yes, my phone's right here," Vanessa replied. She reached into her purse, pulled it out, and handed it to him. "I noticed a nice little sunroom just off the elevators where you can talk," she added with a conspiratorial wink. "Be sure to tell Ruby we're all holding up just fine. I'll stay right here till you get back."

No sooner had Clinton left, Dr. Conford appeared at Eldon's bedside. He was a stout man, early forties, Vanessa guessed.

"When can I talk to my father?" Vanessa asked him. "In a while. Don't disturb him now. I doubt if he's slept this well in weeks. When he awakens, you can visit briefly, but take care not to tire him."

Nodding, Vanessa noted that the pallor in her father's face nearly matched the whiteness of the two pillows supporting his head. He was receiving oxygen through a nasal cannula and his medications through an intravenous drip. As she continued to watch him, a solitary tear wetted her cheek.

"Yes, Dad. Do rest," she murmured as the doctor hurried from the room. There were so many words that needed to be spoken—reminders of her love for him, her appreciation for the devotion and nurturing he and Mama had given Andy and herself.

Wearily she sank down into a chair next to his bed and stared unseeingly at a spot on the opposite wall. It was already past midnight. Her body and mind felt weighted with fatigue.

"Vanessa. Kitten. Look at me."

Her gaze darted to his face. A trembling smile hovered on his lips. His eyes were fixed solidly on hers and a little of his former robust color had risen back into his cheeks.

"Dad! You're awake," she said in a hushed tone. "How . . . how are you feeling?"

"Better."

"Good! You're looking better. Do you know where you are? Do you know what happened to you?" Though her father had been conscious the entire time, she couldn't help but pose the question.

"Yes, kitten." He coughed, then asked weakly. "Where's Clint?"

"Making a phone call. He'll be back soon."

He nodded, closing his eyes. Slowly he opened them again. "What about Lowell? Is he still back home?" She forced herself to meet his inquiring gaze as she explained about Lowell's sudden leaving. Yet all the while, the words nearly stuck in her throat. Could her father read the longing inscribed on her heart? Could he sense how much she loved Lowell? She was certain her need for him was as transparent as the glass of water next to Dad's bedside.

"So the lad's not far away. That's fine. He's a good man, kitten."

"Yes. Yes, he is."

"While we were working together, before I was kidnapped, Lowell asked about you night and day. So many times." Eldon's voice trailed off.

At the sound of his words, her heart twisted. Yes, perhaps Lowell *had* asked, but what good was mere asking? Especially after all that had happened between them. He'd said himself he would never love her. Why had he shown his interest in her? Mere duty, even back then?

"You mustn't try so hard to talk, Dad. You must rest now. The doctor said so."

A spark of determination flashed in his eyes. "I must talk. The sight of my little girl is a sight for sore eyes. That young upstart of a doctor, he's not dry yet behind the ears."

Vanessa held back a smile. Dad certainly hadn't lost his fighting spirit. For that she was grateful.

Another coughing jag wracked Eldon's body. She lifted his head, supporting him with a pillow as he sipped water through a straw. At length, the cough subsided.

"I love you, Dad. Just sleep now. Sleep and get well." She leaned over and kissed his forehead, swallowing back fresh tears.

*****

Sitting inside the Fish and Wildlife Service's headquarters, Lowell gulped down the remainder of his black coffee. It'd been the fourth cup, but so far his usual caffeine fix hadn't kicked in.

He stifled a yawn as he stared at his computer monitor, then clicked on a link to access a website. The colorful images wavered before him and his head throbbed.

What he'd give for a decent night's sleep. He'd struggled through two long nights without more than a few hours, the first while waiting to get the goods on Matt Redding, the second while he'd caught the 1:15 A.M. ferry and finally bedded down at Morrison's guest house. But in those few remaining hours till morning, thoughts of Eldon kept parading through his mind. Lowell found himself getting up still one more time to call the hospital and ask about him.

"Sorry. We can only give out information to family members," the same stern-sounding nurse kept reiterating. Lowell gave his head a quick shake as if shaking off the memory. His only choice now would be to contact Vanessa, who had undoubtedly stayed at Eldon's bedside all night long.

And that choice he quickly rejected.

"More coffee?" the young receptionist asked Lowell as she breezed past his desk and smiled. Sunlight slanting through the window caught highlights of her reddish-brown hair. "Oh, by the way, my name's Millie."

"Pleased to meet you, Millie." Yet before he could accept her offer, his thoughts strayed. He glanced at the clock on the wall, and a sudden picture of another auburn beauty sprang to his mind. No one could hold a match to Vanessa. He thought of her silky flowing hair, those blue-gray eyes that so openly mirrored her emotions, her fierce protectiveness for those she loved.

But most of all, he thought about the feeling of her pressed against him, the passion of her kisses, the fire within himself he could no longer deny. Suddenly if felt so right. There was no room anymore for doubt, kidding himself about some over-inflated sense of duty. He and Vanessa were meant to be together.

Forever.

"Mr. Maxwell?" The sound of Millie's voice brought him back with a start.

"Yes?"

"I said would you care for more coffee?"

"Oh, sorry, but no thanks. "I've had plenty. Too much. Right now I need to clear my head and check in with Morrison."

"He hasn't arrived yet, sir. He called to say he was stalled in traffic on I-5. Said to tell you he'd be there as soon as he could, but it might take a while."

"Morrison should see the freeways in L.A.," Lowell said wryly as he glanced at the clock on the wall. He slumped back down in his chair and propped his feet on his desk, thinking again about Vanessa. Why? Why did he care about her so much? And was it only a matter of caring? Could he truly let go of his own problems and admit the love for her he'd been struggling to deny? Make a lasting commitment to the one woman who'd captured his very soul? The sudden realization jolted him.

"Well, well, Maxwell old boy." Ralph Morrison approached from behind and slapped him on the shoulder.

Lowell sprang to his feet. "Ah, you're here."

"Yes. I've wanted to talk to you. Congratulate you again for a job well done."

"I had lots of backups, don't forget. The other agents on the task force, the sheriff's department on the island, not to mention your help too."

Morrison dropped a leather briefcase on the desk, snapped it open, and produced a stack of papers. "We counted one hundred eighty-nine sea otter carcasses. They're being held right here in our seizure room till the courts authorize their release."

Lowell let out a whistle. "I expected it'd be close to that."

"Have you heard anything about Mr. Paris? Any news about how he's doing?"

"Nope. I tried calling several times, but no one would tell me anything substantial."

Morrison narrowed his gaze on Lowell and frowned. "You look awful."

"Thanks, pal."

"No, Maxwell. I mean it. Take the day off and get some sleep. I should have known better than to insist you start work so soon."

"But there's still too much paper work to finish."

"Maxwell."

"Yes?"

"I thought I made myself perfectly clear. Forget the paper work and get out of here."

Less than an hour later, Lowell had driven back to the guest house and gone straight to bed. Yet he'd only managed to sleep for a few hours, and he couldn't drift back.

He gave the bed sheets one more yank as he flipped over on his side. The room-darkening shades in the room were tightly drawn. He'd turned his cell phone off. So what was the problem? Maybe he was too wired. That happened sometimes. Going so long without sleep, you'd passed the point of no return. But before, he'd always managed to snap back in record time.

Once again he couldn't quiet his restless thoughts. What had Vanessa learned about Eldon? What if her father *did* die?

He pushed himself up on one elbow and hung his feet over the side of the bed, mulling it over as he stared at his cell phone. He couldn't keep taking no for an answer. He had to call the hospital one more time.

He turned the phone back on and punched in the numbers. Drumming his fingers on the bedside table, he listened to the succession of rings on the other end. What was taking so long? At last the operator at the hospital switchboard answered and transferred his call.

"Fifth floor. Ms. Scheller, ward clerk, speaking."

"Who did you say you are?" Lowell asked. "A nurse?" He couldn't help feeling like a blundering fool.

"I'm Ms. Scheller, the ward clerk," she repeated evenly. "How may I help you?"

"I need to talk to a nurse! The nurse in charge of Eldon Paris."

"Are you a family member?"

There it was again. That same lousy question. "Yes," he lied, his voice rising. "His son-in-law!"

Quickly he clenched his jaw, taken aback at his own words. What had made him say that? Was it because deep inside he longed for it to be true?

"Please hold," the ward clerk replied.

"Okay, but hurry." Lowell heaved a sigh. *Family,* he thought. *The Paris family.* Vanessa's image once again came to him—and this time it refused to leave. The thought of the possible family ties tugged inside his gut.

The line remained silent. He tapped his foot impatiently as the minutes wore on. Then he lost the connection. Blasted phone! He knew the cell coverage was sometimes iffy there on the islands, but what a lousy time to be cut off.

Raking a hand through his hair, he started getting dressed. Next he would hurry to the hospital. He'd go straight to Eldon's bedside and say what he needed to say—even if someone tried to kick him out.

And if going there meant he might have to face Vanessa again, so be it. If the news about Eldon was bad, at least he'd be there for her. He couldn't let her experience grief in the same way he had. No, he simply could not.

*****

Vanessa stood outside her father's hospital room, crying softly, when rapid footsteps in the hallway caused her to look up.

Her breath caught, whisper soft. "Lowell!"

He was back, just as she'd dreaded, yet her love for him made her head reel.

He rushed up to her, alarm registering on his face.

"Vanessa. What is it?" he asked. "Why on earth are you crying? Is it bad news? Isn't Eldon going to make it?"

"It looks as if he's going to be fine!" More tears streamed down her face. "I'm crying because I'm happy. And relieved . . . so relieved. The doctor just told us he's certain the crisis is over. The fluid on Dad's lung is clearing. His heart rhythm has returned to normal and his temperature has been down for several hours."

"Thank God," he said, his voice thick with emotion. "I knew Eldon would pull through. He just had to." He reached out and touched her shoulder. "You must be exhausted."

"Yes. Uncle Clint and I both are," she admitted. "Right now he's on the phone again, telling the good news to Ruby"

"Is Eldon sleeping?" Lowell asked.

"He just woke up."

"I need to talk to him. Alone."

"The staff might not let you go in. Only family members are allowed."

"Fine. So consider me family. I might as well be, you know . . ."

She bit her lower lip. "What about your job? Why aren't you at the Wildlife headquarters?"

"Morrison insisted I take the rest of the day off. I'll explain more later after I talk with Eldon."

"All right." She gave a tentative nod as he brushed her side to enter the room. The musky scent of his after-shave tugged at her. What dreadful timing. Why couldn't he have come later? Later, after she and Clinton had ferried back to the islands. This time, saying good-bye would be even more heart-wrenching. Maybe she should leave right now so she wouldn't have to face him again.

Yet she couldn't.

The wait while Lowell and Dad talked seemed an eternity. She must've skimmed through at least a half a dozen magazines, not comprehending a word. She must've downed at least another half dozen cups of coffee from the courtesy refreshment cart in the corner of the waiting room. At last she got to her feet and wandered to the large aquarium in the hallway to watch a family of black striped fish.

"Eldon's in excellent spirits," Lowell said, jolting her from her thoughts as he reappeared at her side.

"Another sure sign of his recovery," she agreed, trying to control her escalating pulse rate. She hesitated. "Well? Did you get to tell Dad everything you planned to?"

"Uh-huh. And even more than I'd planned. Your father's one terrific guy, Nessie. And he keeps getting more terrific all the time."

She was tempted to ask him exactly what Eldon had said, but her better judgment held her back. Lowell's widening grin, the look of tranquility illuminating his face, told her all she needed to know. At long last, Lowell had learned how to let go of his guilt.

He caught her hand. "Nessie?"

"Yes?"

"Could we go somewhere? Just you and I?"

"But why?"

"You'll see." He tightened his grip. "Just come."

In a rooftop garden just off the fifth floor, a garden with lush greenery and fountains and roses the texture of velvet, Vanessa and Lowell sat talking.

"I love you, Nessie," he said without preamble, turning to fix his gaze on hers. "I can't believe I'm hearing myself say this, but I am, and it feels terrific."

At the sound of his words, her stomach knotted. "Please, Lowell. Please don't say it, just because I said it to you." She withdrew her hand from his, fearing where their conversation might be leading. "If what you really want to tell me is good-bye again, please just do it and get it over with."

He turned and faced her, his dark blue eyes imploring. The heady fragrance of the roses wafted about them. "I'm not trying to tell you good-bye. At least not if it's left up to me. Please just give me a chance to explain."

She nodded, too choked up for words. How could she refuse him? How, when she loved him more than she ever dreamed possible?

"As you know, when I first came to the lodge, I was in a bad way," he began, his voice ragged. "Then you came along and complicated my life even further. I knew from the first moment I saw you again, I wanted to make you mine. But loving you, knowing I couldn't offer you any solid future, a future for the kids we might have some day, just about tore my gut in two."

"No wonder," she replied, holding his gaze. "No wonder after what you've been through."

"Then last week when I needed to talk to Morrison, and you hurried to meet Carmen, it seemed to me we'd come to a crossroads. Each of us was responding to our own separate work in our own separate ways. For me, the gap between us grew even wider, and that's when I knew I finally had to tell you what happened back in L.A. I decided once and for all—or so I thought—I was the wrong man to be your husband and the father of your children. I simply wasn't ready to take any more risks, Nessie. That was the bottom line."

"And neither was I," she reminded him. "At least, not at first. You represented to me everything that spelled danger—and loss. And I wasn't ready to open myself to that pain again, especially with Dad's fate still hanging in the balance."

"Yes." One corner of his mouth quirked. "You made that quite clear. So what changed your mind?"

"Something happened that afternoon we went sailing." She sighed deeply, unexpectedly cleansed by the sound of her own confession. "Though I'd been fighting the temptation to fall in love with you, I knew I couldn't fight it any longer. Maybe it was that romantic picnic lunch you prepared or going back again to Iffleman Island or building the sandcastle and watching it wash away." She paused, darting him a smile. "Or maybe it was your kisses. Maybe it was all those things."

His eyes caressed her with a teasing awareness. "So I was that irresistible, huh?"

"Yes." She chuckled. "Oh, yes. But I tried to kid myself that my feelings for you were nothing but an illusion, as temporary as that beautiful day itself. Still, my love for you kept growing and I simply couldn't hold back telling you."

"Ah, Nessie." Before she could utter one more word, he'd gathered her in his arms, his lips crushing hers. "I do love you so," he said huskily, finally releasing her. "Believe me. I want this to be a new beginning, not a good-bye. I'm ready to risk again. I'm ready to move on."

"And I think we've both discovered that without risks, there *is* no living," she replied softly.

He turned, cupped her face in his large hands and planted a quick peck on the tip of her nose. "Without *you,* darling, there is no living. Will you marry me, Nessie? Will you say yes?" Dropping his hands, his words spilled out in a torrent of emotion. "We can find a nice little place somewhere in Seattle, half way between the university and the wildlife headquarters. And while each morning, we'll go our separate ways, we'll have each other to come home to. As often as we can, we'll bring our kids back to the islands. We'll show them how to build sandcastles and dig for clams and go fishing and sailing."

"Oh, Lowell, I love you so much."

"So that means, yes? You'll marry me?"

"Of course!"

This time his kiss was more wonderful, more wildly intoxicating than before.

"Let's hurry and find Clinton," she exclaimed a minute later. She could still feel her pulse racing, the warm flush of her face. "Let's tell my uncle there's even more news to phone home!"

He flashed her a grin. "Before Clinton calls anyone, I think we should talk to your father. This time, together."

"You want to do it the old-fashioned way? You want to ask for my hand in marriage?"

"Too late, my love. I've already taken care of that." The corners of his eyes crinkled as his smile grew wider. "But now we mustn't keep Eldon waiting for your answer."

Epilogue

The double wedding was cozy and intimate that early December evening at Kaloch Bay Lodge. In the lobby where the ceremony was about to begin, arrangements of red and white poinsettias were clustered about the base of the A-shaped candelabra. From it a pyramid of tiny white lights flickered. Boughs of evergreens adorned the windows, wafting forth a sweet, woodsy aroma.

As Vanessa stood in the foyer next to her father, waiting for the ceremony to begin, she looked down at her mother's white Bible she'd chosen to carry in place of a bouquet. How proud and happy Mama would be right now. Andy too.

Over the past months, Eldon had steadily regained his health and zest for living. Now his sparkling blue eyes met Vanessa's. "You're beautiful, kitten," he whispered. "Absolutely beautiful."

"Thank you, Dad." Vanessa's eyes misted as she tucked a delicately gloved hand beneath the fold of his arm. "I love you."

Ruby was the picture of serenity as she stood on Eldon's other side wearing a pastel pink gown edged in lace. Eldon had heartily agreed to give both Vanessa and Ruby away.

Lowell had never appeared more handsome. Standing tall and strong, the last shades of an Indian summer tan contrasting his white tuxedo, his eyes met hers and he smiled. In his lapel he wore a single pink miniature rose, the same roses Vanessa had chosen for the garland crowning her head.

Vanessa's heart swelled with love. Love for Lowell. Love for family. She blinked twice to make sure it wasn't a dream, then turned her gaze on her husband-to-be who waited in front of the stone fireplace with Clinton and the minister.

Friends were filling nearly every folding chair in the lobby. The soft murmur of the guest's conversations mingled with the sounds of the cello player, who'd begun tuning her instrument. The cellist Clinton had volunteered to solicit, Vanessa thought with a smile. Next to Lowell and herself, of course, Ruby and Clinton had appeared the happiest engaged couple Vanessa had known for a long time.

After the last guest was seated, the musician lifted her bow to the strings and the rich swells of "Mediation from Thais" began.

"Considered by some to be the most romantic love song in the world." Ruby's words again floated across Vanessa's memory. And today, on their special day, nothing but the most romantic would do.

The music soon ended, and a hush fell over the room. Then, in the space of a heartbeat, the "Bridal Chorus" from Lohengrin filled the room. Vanessa held Eldon's arm more tightly as the threesome started up the aisle. Wonderingly she lifted her gaze to Lowell. He was staring into her face, sending her tender looks of love.

In minutes the minister intoned the age-old words:

"Dearly beloved, we are gathered together here in the sight of God, and in the face of this company . . ."

Again her heart spilled over with love. Love that would endure. For now and all time.

The End

Don't miss out!

Visit the website below and you can sign up to receive emails whenever Sydell Lowell Voeller publishes a new book. There's no charge and no obligation.

https://books2read.com/r/B-A-KKZY-PDXMC

Also by Sydell Lowell Voeller

Her Sister's Keeper
The Heart Leads Home
The Fisherman's Daughter

Watch for more at sydellvoeller.com.

About the Author

Sydell Lowell Voeller grew up in Edmonds, Washington, and has lived in Forest Grove, Oregon for many years. Her family consists of a husband, two grown sons and their wives, and four grandchildren.

Sydell has been a violinist in semiprofessional orchestras, a registered nurse, and a writing instructor for the LongRidge Writer's Institute. Her interests include reading, camping, astronony, crafting, astronomy, and playing with her two cats.

www.ingramcontent.com/pod-product-compliance
Lightning Source LLC
Chambersburg PA
CBHW061346160726
47995CB00001B/192